"I'm ready to start my life, Austin."

The way his name rolled off her tongue made him want to wrap her in his arms and make her promise she'd never leave. His son needed her. Austin certainly couldn't be a mother to the boy. He barely knew how to be a father. And now Cassie was threatening to abandon them both.

"I don't know what you want me to say." He rubbed the scruff on his chin, trying to figure out a way to change her mind. "I didn't realize you were unhappy here."

"I wasn't. I'm not." She took a few steps his way, pausing at the corner of the laminate counter not far from where he stood. Her fingers traced an imaginary circle on the counter. "I've been happy here. It's been a privilege to take care of AJ. And you've always treated me well. I'm grateful for this job. Please, don't think I'm not."

That eased his tension slightly.

"But I can't do this forever." Her big brown eyes implored him to accept it. Selfishly, he didn't.

Jill Kemerer writes novels with love, humor and faith. Besides spoiling her mini dachshund and keeping up with her busy kids, Jill reads stacks of books, lives for her morning coffee and gushes over fluffy animals. She resides in Ohio with her husband and two children. Jill loves connecting with readers, so please visit her website, jillkemerer.com, or contact her at PO Box 2802, Whitehouse, OH 43571.

Books by Jill Kemerer

Love Inspired

Wyoming Ranchers

The Prodigal's Holiday Hope
A Cowboy to Rely On
Guarding His Secret
The Mistletoe Favor
Depending on the Cowboy
The Cowboy's Little Secret

Wyoming Sweethearts

Her Cowboy Till Christmas
The Cowboy's Secret
The Cowboy's Christmas Blessings
Hers for the Summer

Wyoming Cowboys

The Rancher's Mistletoe Bride
Reunited with the Bull Rider
Wyoming Christmas Quadruplets
His Wyoming Baby Blessing

Visit the Author Profile page at LoveInspired.com for more titles.

The Cowboy's Little Secret

Jill Kemerer

LOVE INSPIRED

INSPIRATIONAL ROMANCE

LOVE INSPIRED®

INSPIRATIONAL ROMANCE

ISBN-13: 978-1-335-58575-2

The Cowboy's Little Secret

Copyright © 2023 by Ripple Effect Press, LLC

For questions and comments about the quality of this book, please contact us at CustomerService@Harlequin.com.

Love Inspired
22 Adelaide St. West, 41st Floor
Toronto, Ontario M5H 4E3, Canada
www.LoveInspired.com

Printed in U.S.A.

Blessed is the man that trusteth in the Lord, and whose hope the Lord is. For he shall be as a tree planted by the waters, and that spreadeth out her roots by the river, and shall not see when heat cometh, but her leaf shall be green; and shall not be careful in the year of drought, neither shall cease from yielding fruit.

—*Jeremiah 17:7–8*

Thank you to the Love Inspired editors,
especially Shana Asaro and Melissa Endlich,
who graciously allowed me to write the
Wyoming Ranchers series.
I'm blessed to work with you.

Chapter One

This was the toughest decision he'd had to make in years, and time was running out. If he didn't come up with a plan for the cattle soon, the entire herd would be vulnerable this winter. There was no way he could feed them all.

Austin Watkins opened the side door to his farmhouse with a tad too much force. Inside the mudroom, he took off his boots before running hot water to wash his hands. He stared out the window above the utility sink as he lathered his forearms with soap. The yellowing lawn practically shouted drought. Summer was over. Maybe not officially, but since it was the first day of September in Wyoming, it might as well be.

Where had he gone wrong?

Austin had been in charge of the ranch for over a decade, and he'd never experienced conditions this dry. The hay harvest had been pathetic, and the pastures lacked adequate forage for his cattle to graze this winter. Unlike a few of his closest buddies, he didn't have access to thousands of acres of land.

His cattle would starve.

The ranch would go bankrupt.

And he and little AJ would be out on the streets.

After flicking off the faucet, he grabbed the hand towel and dried off. There was no getting around it. He needed to sell some of the cattle. He'd put it off long enough. But thinning the herd would merely solve one problem while creating another.

How would the ranch survive *next* year with fewer cows?

Anxiety slammed against his chest, and he could barely inhale a full breath. He forced himself to close his eyes as he slowly counted to ten. The process only marginally held back his fears. A knot of inevitable failure grew larger and more tangled each day.

God, where are You? Why won't You help?

"Austin?" Cassie's voice carried from the other room.

He pulled himself together. Not only did the cattle depend on him, people did, too. He didn't have the luxury of falling apart. Not this time.

Austin strode through the doorway, stopping short at the sight of Cassie Berber sitting on a stool at the counter of the eat-in U-shaped kitchen and sipping a cup of tea. Her brown hair fell in waves over her shoulders and down her back. She was reading something on her phone. At twenty-six, the nanny was way too young for him, but even if she were closer to his thirty-three years of age, he couldn't pursue a relationship with her. He'd only let her down, too.

"Oh, good, you're here." Her brown eyes shimmered with flecks of gold. She had the whitest teeth he'd ever seen, and her high cheekbones made her look like a model. Yep, Cassie was a beauty. And he'd been fighting his attraction to her for months.

"What do you need?" He couldn't help the fact that he sounded gruff. Being around her, seeing that smile, watching how caring she was with his son—it was getting to him.

Maybe he'd been single for too long. He hadn't dated in years. Wasn't planning on changing that, either.

He didn't want it coming out that AJ wasn't his biological child. Not too many women would understand his relationship with Camila, the boy's late mother, and he couldn't imagine sharing the details of how they met or why he agreed to be named the father on AJ's birth certificate.

His brother, Randy, was the only person who knew the truth about the boy. Last year, Austin had gone down to Texas for a week and had come home with a three-month-old baby. Folks around here assumed he'd had a girlfriend in Texas, gotten her pregnant and was raising AJ—Austin Junior—because she'd died.

He hadn't set them straight and wasn't going to. It was none of their business. Plus, he couldn't take the chance—miniscule as it was—that the man Camila didn't want raising her son would somehow learn the truth.

Cassie set her phone down, then clasped her hands on the counter, meeting his gaze once more.

He waited for her to speak, but silence thickened the air. Was this about AJ? At eighteen months, the boy saw no point in walking when he could run. Those chubby legs could cover a lot of ground in a very short time. The kid was curious, too. A handful, that one. A cute handful. Austin loved the boy with every bit of his heart.

"I don't know how to say this." Cassie's eyebrows formed a V. His gut tightened as he prepared for bad news. "But well…it's time I moved on."

Moved on. The words hovered between them. He felt as if he could pluck them both out of the air and arrange them on the counter. They unnerved him, upended the secure part of his world.

His two priorities were the ranch and AJ.

And now both were being threatened.

"Come again?" He was proud he managed to sound as calm as he did. Maybe he'd heard her incorrectly or was misunderstanding what she said.

"Now that Gramps is gone…" She stared at her hands. Her knuckles grew white from gripping her fingers so tightly. "It doesn't make sense to stay in Sunrise Bend any longer."

"Says who?"

She met his gaze, and her eyes pleaded with him to understand. Well, he didn't. He didn't comprehend at all.

"It's time," she said quietly. "I only moved back to help Mom take care of him. It's been a few months since the funeral. I'm ready for my own place."

"Okay, so let's find you an apartment." If she was tired of living with her mother, they could remedy that in a weekend.

Her sad smile slipped away as quickly as it appeared. "It's not just that. I have a degree I'd like to put to use."

What was her degree in again? He couldn't remember. It probably wouldn't help matters if he admitted that at this point.

"Don't you like taking care of AJ?" It was a cheap shot, but he'd appeal to her loving nature. He could *not* lose her as a nanny. She was reliable, energetic and patient with his baby. Cassie was practically a mother to the child.

His breathing grew shallow, a sure sign his stress levels were escalating.

"Of course, I love him. You know that. Don't twist this around to something it isn't." Indignant anger burst like sparks around her as she got off the stool.

"Then what is it?" He tossed off her comments about living on her own and wanting to use her degree. There was more to it—wasn't there?

"I told you." She stood tall, hitching her head to the side. "I'm ready for my own life. I moved here to help with Gramps. I'm thankful I was able to spend his final year with him. But I never planned on living with my mom or being a nanny for this long. I'm ready to start my life, Austin."

The way his name rolled off her tongue made him want to wrap her in his arms and make her promise she'd never leave. His son needed her. Austin certainly couldn't be a mother to the boy. He barely knew how to be a father. And now Cassie was threatening to abandon them both.

"I don't know what you want me to say." He rubbed the scruff on his chin, trying to figure out a way to change her mind. "I didn't realize you were unhappy here."

"I wasn't. I'm not." She took a few steps his way, pausing at the corner of the laminate counter not far from where he stood. Her fingers traced an imaginary circle on the counter. "I've been happy here. It's been a privilege to take care of AJ. And you've always treated me well. I'm grateful for this job. Please don't think I'm not."

That eased his tension slightly.

"But I can't do this forever." Her big brown eyes implored him to accept that. Selfishly, he didn't.

He wanted her to stay forever, for nothing to change. He wanted to come into the kitchen every afternoon when AJ was napping and find Cassie sitting on the same stool, sipping her tea, scrolling through her phone. He wanted to leave the daily hours of raising his son in her expert hands.

Couldn't just one thing in his life be uncomplicated?

"I'll stay until the end of September." She licked her lips, not meeting his eyes. "A month should give you enough time to find a new nanny."

One month? A new nanny?

His lungs compressed. The walls seemed to be closing in on him, and he almost thrust his hand out to grip the counter for balance.

He couldn't move. Couldn't think. Couldn't process what was happening. *No, not again.*

He'd frozen like this the day Randy found Dad dead from a heart attack when Austin was twenty-one years old.

He'd frozen again the night Camila, AJ's mother, had saved his life when she probably should have left him to die.

And here he was again, a marble statue, facing disaster and unable to do a thing about it.

His world was imploding, and all he could do was just stand there.

Cassie grew concerned as the blood drained from Austin's face. She hadn't expected him to be upset. She'd worked for the handsome rancher for well over a year. He was reserved, take-charge and a loving father to his son. He was also intimidating and hard to read. When she'd rehearsed what she was going to say, she never imagined he'd respond beyond a *thank you for your service* and *we'll find a new nanny in no time.*

"Austin?" She barely recognized her high-pitched voice. "Are you okay?"

Color rushed to his face, and he blinked two, three times, then strode past her to the table, where he grabbed a chair and took a seat with jerky movements.

"No, Cassie, I'm not okay." His eyes—gray with a hint of blue—met hers. Guilt flared at the turbulence within them. "You're what keeps this part of my life together. I'm already trying to make decisions about my cows, and no matter what, I'm bound to fail. I can't feed the entire herd this winter. I just can't. The cost of everything's rising…and now you're telling me I need to find a new nanny? And I have one month to do it?"

Cassie joined him at the table and sat across from him. He was flexing his fingers, then curling them into his palms again and again. Sympathy tempted her to cover those restless hands with her own, but she didn't dare.

She'd had no idea he was dealing with all that. Had no clue he put so much stock in her babysitting skills with AJ. Maybe there was more to the self-reliant rancher than she thought. "I'll help you find a nanny if you'd like."

"I don't want your help. I want you to stay." The sharpness in his tone caught her off guard, and once again, she barely recognized the man in front of her. The Austin she knew never lost his temper with her, never rose his voice. He barked out orders to everyone except her and AJ. With them, he was gentle and kind, and he even smiled on occasion.

His closed-off personality had been one of the reasons she'd thrived here as AJ's nanny. It had kept her from romanticizing Austin. She tended to be attracted to the older, more mature type. Her father-figure issues had gotten her into trouble before, and she'd learned her lesson the hard way. She wouldn't—couldn't—make a similar mistake again.

When she did decide to start dating, she would only consider someone her own age. Someone who would treat her like an equal. And if she couldn't find him? She'd remain single, which might be easier said than done.

For the past couple of months, every time she'd found herself staring at the man in front of her—all six-foot-one-inches of lean muscle—she'd had to remind herself he was off-limits. Sure, his short light brown hair tempted her to touch it, and the trimmed scruff on his perfectly chiseled face only added to his appeal. Those weren't the things that attracted her to him, though.

It was his maturity, his take-charge nature. She'd been a sucker for those traits since she was young.

Sadly, the "mature" man who'd cured her of her daddy issues had also left her shattered.

Austin Watkins was someone to look at and not touch. And since he'd never once given her the slightest indication that he found her attractive or wanted a relationship beyond a professional one, she'd zipped up her heart and glued it shut for good measure.

It hadn't been difficult. She'd been focused on her grandfather's declining health and on the joy of watching AJ's first milestones. One of those milestones was partially responsible for her decision to quit.

She loved the boy too much. And he'd started calling her mama. Her heart practically seized every time he said it, even when she'd point to her chest and say "Cassie." The child refused to call her anything but mama.

Oh, how she wished she really were his mother. If she

didn't walk away now, she'd never be able to, and that wouldn't be fair to any of them.

"Do you have a job lined up?" Austin's low voice startled her.

"No, not yet."

"Where are you looking?"

She shrugged, giving him an apologetic smile, even though she wasn't sure what she was apologizing for. "Colorado, but I haven't seriously started researching jobs yet."

"So there's a chance you'll stay?" His eyes lit with hope, and it was all she could do not to tell him what he wanted to hear.

"I don't think so."

"But if you don't have a job…"

"I'll find one." She straightened her shoulders, proud of herself for standing her ground.

"Well, if you can't find one right away, you can stay on for as long as you want."

She shook her head. "My final day will be September thirtieth. It's a Friday." She'd already noted it.

"Why are you so adamant about quitting?" His face fell, and regret slid all the way down to her toes.

Why? Because she'd done what she'd moved here to do. She'd helped take care of her grandfather. Together, she and her mother had kept Gramps out of a nursing home, allowing him to finish out his days in a familiar setting. And since the funeral two months ago, Cassie had grown envious of her friends who all had good jobs and nice apartments. Some of them had even gotten engaged.

Meanwhile, here she was, babysitting full-time, living with her mom, with no expectation of having the life she'd dreamed about when attending university in Colorado Springs. If she didn't take charge of her life now, she'd wind up unemployed the second AJ became a teenager, and she'd still be living with her mom with no prospects of her own. The thought was depressing.

"Hey, don't worry," she said lightly. "Like I said, I'll help you find a new nanny. And I know you'll figure out what to do about the ranch."

"Couldn't you find a job around here? Maybe something part-time? Then you could watch AJ in the mornings or afternoons."

He really wasn't giving up on this, was he?

Cassie slid her hand behind her neck to hook her hair over one shoulder. She wanted to believe he was asking her these questions because he thought she was a good nanny. But the realistic side of her knew it was because her quitting would disrupt his life.

"I want to use my business degree." How could she explain without sounding arrogant? "I always saw myself helping a company grow and be profitable."

He sighed as he considered her words. "Sunrise Bend has businesses."

"Yeah, mostly family-owned. I can't think of anyone looking to hire a manager."

He opened his mouth to say something, must have thought better of it and closed it again.

She didn't want to manage a family-owned business here, anyway. She wanted to move closer to her friends, get an apartment where she could walk to the coffee shop each morning and have a job where she dressed professionally. She wanted to feel important for once.

Had she ever felt important? Even one day in her life?

Before moving back to Sunrise Bend, she'd been

working two part-time jobs in Colorado Springs to make ends meet while she looked for a permanent position. Her job search had not gone well. The few people who'd interviewed her had all said the same thing—she lacked experience. How was she supposed to get experience if no one would hire her?

"Why don't you think it over more?" Austin asked. "There's no hurry. No rush."

Easy for him to say.

"I'm twenty-six. I'm not getting any younger."

"Twenty-six, bah." He waved it off like it was nothing. "You have your whole life ahead of you."

"Yeah, I do, and I'd like to get started on it."

That shut him up.

"Have you thought about how AJ will be affected?" He didn't sound angry; defeated was more like it.

And he wasn't playing fair. Of course, she worried about the boy.

"Yes, I have thought about how he'll be affected, and trust me, this will be best for him, too."

"How can you say that?"

"Because he's too attached to me, Austin. And I'm too attached to him. It's better this way. He calls me mama, and I'm not his mother."

His shoulders softened. Occasionally, she'd wondered about the boy's mother. Austin didn't strike her as the love 'em and leave 'em type, but by all accounts, that's what he'd done. Did he regret it? Or had he loved AJ's mother but the feeling hadn't been returned? There were a lot of unanswered questions regarding Austin's past, and they'd remain a mystery as far as she was concerned. Getting answers would only lead to trouble.

"In time, you'll see I'm right." She stood, grabbing her

phone, and strode to the other end of the kitchen counter where her purse had fallen on its side. Hoisting it over her shoulder, she turned back to him. "I'll start looking for a new nanny on Monday."

Not waiting for his response, she headed through the mudroom and out the door. Jogged down the steps of the side porch and marched straight to her white Honda Civic. The car had gotten her through a decade of driving, and it only had a few rust spots above the rear tire wells.

Another reason to get a good job—it would allow her to buy a newer vehicle. And pay off her student loans. And fly to the beach for a real vacation. And start a retirement fund. And...

Live life on her terms.

Be proud of herself.

But it would come at a cost. Because regardless of what Austin thought, she did love AJ. And leaving him was going to break her heart.

That's why it was better for her to quit now. Before it became impossible to leave.

She'd announced she was quitting and...walked out? Austin stared open-mouthed in the direction of the mudroom and flinched at the sound of the door shutting. She hadn't stayed so they could discuss it more? So he could talk her out of leaving?

He lumbered to his feet and went over to the sink. Poured a glass of water and took a drink before setting the glass down. He gripped the counter's edge with both hands, grinding his teeth together as he tried to make sense of what had just happened.

Cassie was quitting. She wanted to start her life—

whatever that meant. And then she had the audacity to claim it would be better for AJ? How in the world would losing the only mother figure he'd ever known possibly be good for the kid?

The side door creaked, and he straightened. Maybe she'd realized what a terrible idea quitting was and changed her mind.

"Hey, what's up?" Randy waltzed inside with Ned, the service dog for his heart condition, trotting next to him. His brother grabbed a handful of grapes from the bowl on the counter and began popping them in his mouth one by one. The black Lab sat, wagging his tail.

His little brother was a few inches shorter than him. They shared the same light brown hair and had been told they had the same smile. Austin would be the first to admit he wasn't much of a smiler, while easygoing Randy grinned often.

"Is this a bad time?" Randy asked. "You look like you caught someone stealing your cattle."

Austin shook off his foul mood. He didn't ask for help often, but this was one of those times he'd have to suck it up. He needed all the help he could get.

"Cassie's quitting."

Randy choked on a grape, thumping his chest with his fist. Ned nudged his nose against Randy's free hand. When he stopped sputtering, he stroked the dog's head.

"You done?" Austin asked. That had been unnecessarily dramatic. He motioned his fingers for them to move to the living room. Randy took a seat in the recliner, while Austin perched on the edge of the couch.

"Why is she quitting?" he asked. Then he gave one final cough.

"I don't know. Some mumble-jumble about starting

over and moving on now that her grandfather passed." He thrust his fingers into his hair. He was tempted to grip it and yank a clump out.

"Hmm." Randy's head wobbled as if he understood.

"What? Don't act like this makes sense."

"She only came back to town to help her mom with her grandfather. She never hid the fact."

"Well, what good does that do me now?"

"Hey, at least you had her for this long."

"You're not helping." Austin clamped his mouth shut before he gave in to the urge to start shouting. No sense waking up AJ. The boy still had a good hour of naptime left, and he wasn't going to cut it short by letting his temper get the best of him.

"What are you going to do now?" Randy asked.

"Convince her to stay."

"Come on." His brother arched his left eyebrow.

"I mean it. Who else could I trust with my son? He needs her. Loves her. Depends on her."

"That's not really fair to Cassie, though."

Austin glared at him. "Are you on my side or not?"

"This isn't about taking sides. You're not seeing straight because it's going to be a big hassle for you to find a new babysitter."

He could say that again. Austin sank deeper into the couch with his legs sprawled. He looked around the room. The old farmhouse was just that…old. He and Randy had grown up here with their dad. Their mother had died of pneumonia when Austin was four and Randy was two. Neither of them had clear memories of her. And in the years since she'd died, the house had grown dated, in need of a renovation.

For a long time, he'd toyed with the idea of replacing the flooring and putting in a new kitchen. Probably should have done it long ago. He couldn't afford to now. At least the place was comfortable. Fit like a glove, really. But it looked worse for wear, kind of like how he felt. Worn down. Past its prime.

"I'll have Hannah put the word out around town that you need a new nanny."

"Cassie said she'd help me find one." Maybe he should resign himself to the fact she was leaving.

"Between the two of them, they'll hook you up with the perfect babysitter in no time. And hey, tomorrow night is Mac's bachelor party. It will take your mind off your troubles."

Who cared about a bachelor party at a time like this?

Austin didn't bother responding. He couldn't afford to take his mind off his troubles. And he certainly didn't want another babysitter, perfect or not. He wanted Cassie.

She knew what AJ needed. Everything ran smoothly with her in charge. She didn't make demands on Austin's time, showed up when she said she would and was the main reason AJ was reaching his developmental milestones.

What was Austin going to do without her?

If he'd thought his life was on the verge of collapse before talking to her this afternoon, it had since slid to the edge of the abyss.

The ranch. The cattle. AJ.

Nothing else mattered.

He'd find a way to deal with it all. He had to. There were no other options.

Chapter Two

❧

"One more week, man." Austin raised his hand to Mac Tolbert for a high five the following afternoon. Mac grinned, pulling him in for a side hug. Austin was more than willing to fake enthusiasm about this bachelor party for the sake of one of his best friends. Besides, no one needed his sad-sack stories about Cassie leaving or the ranch failing. He was used to handling his problems on his own. "You nervous?"

"Me?" Mac jabbed his thumb into his chest. "Of course, I'm nervous. I can't believe it's almost here. Some days it feels like I just met Bridget, and other days I feel like I've been waiting twenty years to marry her. I'm ready for the wedding."

They stood outside Mac's stables as the rest of their friends joined them. Randy was there, naturally, as well as Sawyer Roth and the Mayer brothers, Jet and Blaine. The six of them had been best buddies most of their lives, and they'd all been single until recently. At this point, Austin was the only unattached one left.

"Is everybody ready to saddle up?" Mac asked the group.

They'd opted to ride horses out to a tree-lined creek where they used to camp when they were younger. It would be like old times, eating supper next to the campfire and hanging out under a sky full of stars. Instead of camping this go-round, though, they would all be returning to their houses to sleep. It seemed they had more responsibilities and people to go home to now.

Until yesterday, Austin had been looking forward to this excursion with the boys. He'd hired a teenager to babysit AJ tonight, but he was plagued with stress over Cassie leaving, and when his mind didn't fixate on the nanny issue, it switched to the cattle problem.

He could really use a night off from his worries.

Austin listened with half an ear as the guys joked around. Sawyer led the way to the corral where several horses milled about. Mac had insisted they ride his prime horses for the outing. He'd recently inherited his father's large fortune, and he'd always been the most generous guy Austin knew.

It didn't take long for each of them to select their mounts. Soon they were heading down the trail to the campsite. The rolling hills revealed the dry prairie as they made their way toward the stand of trees that led to the creek.

Austin inhaled the clear Wyoming air and tried to find peace in the moment. The blue sky held no clouds. In the distance, a hawk circled, and the clip-clop of hooves on the ground soothed him. This—riding horses, being outdoors, hanging out with the guys—had been a part of him forever.

Sawyer pulled his horse up next to him. "I wanted to tell you Tess found another source of hay. This one's in Ohio."

"Really?" Austin sat up straighter in the saddle. Another source of hay was good news, indeed. "How much do they have?" And could he afford it?

"More than I can pay for at this point." Sawyer gave him the details. "Before I place my order, I thought you might want to buy some, too. Would save us on shipping costs."

It touched him that Sawyer was including him in this. Austin had already bought a small load of hay at triple last year's price from a farm in Missouri, and it hadn't been very good quality. But if it meant keeping his cattle fed, he'd take anything at this point.

"Tess requested a hay analysis. It should be worth the money." Sawyer adjusted the brim of his cowboy hat. "I don't know how I'd manage without her. This hay business...well... I'm busy taking care of the cattle and the ranch itself. Plus, with the baby on the way, it's hard trying to find hay, too."

"Tell me about it." For a moment, he envied his friend. Tess was a sharp businesswoman. She ran her own bookkeeping business, and the ranch was technically hers, so she and Sawyer made all the decisions together.

Ever since his dad died, Austin had been making the ranch decisions. Sure, Randy had helped until he opened the outdoor outfitter store in town, but his brother's heart had never been in ranching. And Austin's was.

Jet looked back over his shoulder at them. "Did I hear something about hay?"

"Tess found a farm in Ohio with a surplus." Sawyer's voice carried.

"Do you think I could get in on that?" Jet asked.

"They have plenty," Sawyer said.

Blaine said something Austin couldn't make out, and the mood picked up all around.

"How's Tess feeling?" She was due with their baby in December. Tucker, her almost-four-year-old son from a previous marriage, couldn't wait for his sibling to arrive.

"Great. Now that I got smart and stocked the freezer with a variety of ice-cream flavors, life has improved. This cooler weather should help, too."

They continued to catch up until they reached the campsite. Mac had instructed his ranch hands to bring firewood and supplies there earlier. A large circle for the bonfire had been cleared and a stack of freshly chopped wood stood nearby. Coolers full of drinks and food rested at the foot of a tree. The spruce trees and pines had already shed brown needles in mounds to the ground below them. Water trickled through the creek, shallow as it was.

They dismounted, and after watering the horses and tethering them to picket lines, the guys all got to work starting the fire. Once it was crackling and the flames licked the air, they each grabbed a camping chair and sat around the fire, eating and drinking the refreshments from the coolers.

The talk shifted to the wedding next Saturday. Austin was Mac's best man, and all the other guys were groomsmen. Once they went over the particulars about the rehearsal dinner Friday night and when they needed to be at the church on Saturday, the teasing began.

"Better get prepared, Mac," Randy said. "Hannah wants to plan a trip to Denver and has already insisted you and Bridget come along." He then addressed the rest of the group. "If she had her way, she'd want you all there with us, but she knows it's tough with the babies."

"Holly would jump on that in a heartbeat if she weren't

so sick all the time." Jet grimaced. He and his wife, Holly, had recently found out she was expecting. "I thought they called it morning sickness, not all-day-and-half-the-night sickness. Did Tess throw up all the time, Sawyer?"

Sawyer shook his head. "No, just in the morning, and it only lasted for a few months. She's feeling good now."

"How are Sienna and the baby doing, Blaine?" Mac asked. Blaine looked up from his phone where he'd been typing.

"Sorry. She texted me. I was worried she needed something. Madeline's doing good, and Sienna is feeling better every day. It's been a whirlwind couple of weeks." Sienna and Blaine had fallen in love this summer, despite the obstacles of her being recently divorced and in her third trimester.

Austin took a drink of water and studied each of his friends. They were all paired off at this point. As for him, he didn't want a girlfriend or a wife. Frankly, he considered a romantic relationship one more thing to worry about. Another person who depended on him. Another person he'd only let down. Sometimes, though, he wondered what it would be like to have what his friends had.

They all had partners. Their wives helped them and vice versa. Austin could list plenty of ways the women his friends had married had improved their lives.

Maybe it was the fact he'd grown up without a mother, or maybe it was having to be the man of the house the instant after Dad's heart attack, but he was just now understanding how having a good woman in your life could make a difference.

He frowned, staring at the ground in front of him. Good women were for his friends. Not for him.

He didn't know how to love a woman. Wasn't in tune

with their needs. Had no idea how to read them. As for protecting? He'd laugh if it were funny, but it wasn't. He'd been blindsided by his father's heart attack, and in the process, he'd failed Randy. Worse, he'd fallen into a dark place. Depression. And it had led him down to Texas, to a weekend of being blackout drunk and on the verge of ending it all. To a hole-in-the-wall bar where armed men took over, and instead of being aware of the situation, he'd been in a haze until a stranger had put her own life at risk by dragging him outside to safety.

He owed his life to Camila. He'd never forget it.

The bottom line? When the people he loved needed him the most, he froze. And when he froze, he let them down.

His solution had been to avoid being in that situation in the first place. He hadn't allowed himself to get so close to a woman that he couldn't live without her.

Cassie's pretty smile flashed through his mind. *Not her. Especially not her.*

"What do you say, Austin?" Jet teased.

He shook his head, confused. "What are you talking about?"

"Holly mentioned what a cute couple you and Janelle would make." Jet's cocky grin made Austin want to swipe it right off his face.

"Holly can keep dreaming." His tone may have been too harsh. Jet's guffaws made him think it wasn't harsh enough.

"If you ask me, Austin here should look closer to home." Mac lifted his index finger. "Cassie's already great with AJ, and she's easy on the eyes."

He stilled. Did his friends know he was attracted to

her? He hadn't told anyone. Tried to hide it as much as possible from not only them, but himself as well.

"Cassie?" Randy shook his head, waving as if the idea was ludicrous. "I'm not seeing it."

Austin wasn't, either. But he bristled anyway. Why didn't his own brother think he and Cassie could be together?

Probably because Austin was way too old for her. And too out of touch with what she might need. *Face it, man, you were blindsided by her putting in her notice yesterday. You didn't even know she wanted to get some corporate job. You assumed she'd never leave. You don't know her at all.*

"Why can't you see him with Cassie?" Blaine asked. Austin wanted to give him a fist pump, but Blaine was too far away, and it would give them all the wrong impression.

"I don't know." Randy shrugged. "She only came back to help with her grandfather. And now he's gone."

Austin couldn't argue with that. His own brother understood the situation. Why had he overlooked it, though? Why hadn't he prepared himself better for the fact that she'd eventually leave?

"Randy's right," Austin said. "She put in her notice last night. She's leaving at the end of the month."

They all stared at him with the same perplexed expressions.

"Who's going to watch AJ?" Sawyer asked.

"I don't know." If he didn't change the subject pronto, there was no telling what might come out of his mouth. He might spew all the problems he'd been dealing with, the same way he had with Cassie yesterday. The thought horrified him. "I'll figure it out."

"Where's she going?" Blaine asked.

"Does she have another job or something?" Mac looked confused.

Austin met Randy's gaze. His brother was watching his reaction, and he thought about how vulnerable Randy had been with him last summer when he'd finally told Austin about his heart condition. Maybe it was time to try a bit of transparency himself.

"She wants to put her college degree to use, and she's ready for her own place."

"What's her degree in?" Jet asked.

"Business."

"Bridget's apartment will be free after next week." Mac lifted one shoulder in an easy shrug. "She could live there."

"And there's got to be a job around here she could put the degree to use with," Blaine added.

"But then who would take care of AJ?" Sawyer asked.

That was the problem. He needed her here to take care of AJ, not so she could find her dream job.

Randy stood. "If you want Cassie to stay and take care of AJ, maybe you should get her involved with the ranch, too. The business end, I mean. And you should definitely mention Bridget's apartment."

"I'll take that into consideration." His voice sounded rougher than sandpaper, but he didn't care. They might think they had the solutions to his problems, but he knew better.

Jet had that twinkle in his eyes again. "You'll just have to convince her to stay."

"I'm not convincing anyone about anything," he muttered.

"Well, boys, you know what to do." Jet paused to make

sure he had their attention. "Operation Make Cassie Stay commences immediately. Let's show her Sunrise Bend is where she belongs."

Austin bowed his head and stared at the ground. Their support meant the world to him. And for once, maybe he should take their advice.

He did need Cassie. AJ needed her. And if it meant doing something uncomfortable, like asking for her advice about managing the ranch better, it would be worth it. It didn't mean he was going to take the route the rest of them were on.

Love wasn't in his future. But maybe he could convince Cassie to stick around for his son's sake. It was worth a try.

How was she going to break it to her mom that she was ready to move on?

Cassie looked at her mother sitting across the table from her at Bubba's, a local barbecue joint, on Saturday night. She'd been putting off this conversation for the past couple of weeks, but now that she'd gotten over the hurdle of giving her notice to Austin, it was time to gently ease her mother into the idea.

Was she making a mistake in leaving so soon after Gramps died? The last thing she wanted to do was add to her mother's pain. With Gramps gone, Mom was truly alone. She'd never remarried after Cassie's dad left all those years ago.

If Cassie moved, would her mother be okay?

"It's been a hot minute since I've been here on a Saturday night." Mom smiled, her brown eyes crinkling in the corners. She'd curled her not-quite-shoulder-length brown hair and had on a peasant-style blouse with jeans and slip-on canvas shoes. It had been months since Cassie had seen her mother this put together. Her mom's happy mood only frayed her nerves further.

Cassie took a long drink of her soda as thoughts tumbled around in her head. Mom was finally getting back to herself after a rough couple of years. Was she about to ruin it?

"We need to talk." Her mother reached across the table and took Cassie's hand in hers.

Wasn't that supposed to be her line? Confused, she tried to guess what her mom wanted to discuss. Had she somehow found out she'd told Austin she was quitting? News spread like a brush fire in this town, but she doubted Austin had put the word out for a new nanny already.

"Carlos Fuentes asked me out."

Carlos Fuentes? Cassie sat back, stunned. Mom was… dating? Where had this come from?

And her mother was blushing. Cassie tried to remember if she'd ever dated anyone in the fifteen years after her father left them. She couldn't think of anyone, unless Mom had connected with someone while she was away at college. It was possible. Doubtful, though. Cassie tended to forget Stacy Berber wasn't only her mother but a woman, too.

Mom squeezed her hand. "He's been very kind to me. We work the same shift, and he's been so emotionally supportive ever since your grandfather got worse. So I said yes."

"Why didn't you tell me?" Her mother had been getting close to a man all this time and hadn't seen fit to say anything?

"I didn't know how to, and it wasn't going anywhere

until…" She let go of Cassie's hand and exhaled a soft breath. "After Gramps died, I don't know. I guess it kind of hit me that life is passing me by."

Life is passing me by. Wasn't that exactly what had been going through her own head?

"It's okay, Mom. I don't want you to think I'm upset. I'm not. I want you to be happy, and Carlos seems like a good man." She'd seen him around Sunrise Bend, and he'd always been friendly and kind to her. "I was just taken by surprise, that's all."

"You're not mad, then?"

"No, of course not." She shook her head, smiling. "I think it's great."

She wasn't lying. Her mother deserved more out of life than just a job on the assembly line after years of taking care of Cassie, then Gramps.

"Thanks, Cass. Your approval means the world to me."

They talked about Carlos—a widower with two adult children—for several minutes, and then their food arrived. As Cassie dolloped sour cream on her baked potato, she glanced at her mother, who not only looked content but positively glowed.

In some ways, this was a relief. Mom would be fine if Cassie moved. In fact, with Carlos in the picture, this conversation might go better than she'd dared to hope. But where to start? She didn't know how to broach the topic of moving without hurting her mom's feelings.

"Mom, I have something to tell you, too."

Her mother set her fork down and turned her full attention to her. Those brown eyes sparkled with hope. Why? What did her mom think she was going to say?

"Is this about you and Austin?"

She was taken aback. "There is no *me and Austin*. I've

been thinking a lot about my future, and with Gramps gone, I'm ready to move on." It still hurt to think of her grandfather no longer with them. He'd been such a loving, comforting presence in her life, especially after her father left.

Gramps had been the one who came to her softball games. He'd been the one to take her out driving on country roads while Mom was at work. He'd encouraged her to get her degree, to experience life outside Sunrise Bend. He'd told her time and again that he was proud of her, that the sky was the limit for his Cassie.

She missed him. A lump formed in her throat. She would always miss him.

"Move on?" Her mom seemed to be trying on the concept. Then the corners of her mouth lifted in an understanding smile. "I'm a little surprised."

"You are?"

"Yes, I thought…" She dabbed at her lips with a napkin. "Well, I guess it was wishful thinking."

"About what?" Something told her this was about Austin.

"I know how much you love the baby. You've practically raised AJ at this point. And you and Austin seem to get along well. He really came through for us in those final days with your grandfather."

Cassie averted her gaze. He had. His presence at the hospital had supported both her and her mother. Austin hadn't even needed to say anything. He was just… steady. Rock-solid. The kind of guy who would never let you down.

But she had a history with guys who only let her down, so maybe she was putting him on a pedestal without good reason.

"Yeah, we get along fine." She'd give her mom that. "But I never planned on being a nanny forever. I want to get a job—a real job—and an apartment and hang out with friends and get my life started, you know?"

"I do know, and I don't blame you." Mom's tender expression made it clear she understood. "I can never thank you enough for coming home and putting your life on hold. It meant so much to me. And if Gramps had been more lucid, it would have meant the world to him, too."

"He always knew who I was up until this summer." She'd been thankful the dementia hadn't taken all of his memories away.

"I hate that he went through all of that." Her face fell.

"I hate that we did, too. It was hard on us all."

Their eyes met and understanding flowed between them.

"So where do you want to go? I'm assuming you want to live in a bigger town."

"I'm applying for positions in Colorado. A few of my friends are in Denver. A few are still in Colorado Springs. I'm not picky. I just need a job, preferably in one of those towns so I won't be completely alone, starting from scratch, you know?"

"You'll do great wherever you end up. But I'm sure going to miss you."

Cassie concentrated on buttering her roll. She was going to miss her mom, too.

"When do you think you'll leave?"

"I gave Austin my notice yesterday. My last day is September thirtieth. And I told him I'd help him find a new nanny."

"What if you don't have a new job lined up by then?"

"I'll move anyway. I'll probably go to Colorado

Springs. Take my chances. I can always work a few part-time jobs until I find a full-time one."

Since James—Professor Donovan—was now teaching at a private college in Connecticut, Cassie had no problem returning to Colorado Springs. If he still lived there, though, she would have crossed the town off her list.

Of all the wrong moves she'd made in her life, James had been the biggest mistake.

Her throat tightened uncomfortably thinking about it.

Which was why she didn't think about it. Ever. She'd mentally flogged herself enough over him.

God had helped her through that terrible time. And she'd slowly gotten back to herself.

Find someone your own age. Someone who respects you.

"You know I love having you here, Cass, but if you're set on moving, I'll help. I'm sure Carlos will help, too, if you're comfortable having him around."

Was she comfortable having him around? She didn't know. Maybe if she got to know him better.

"Why don't we play it by ear and invite Carlos over for supper or something?"

Mom's eyes welled with tears. Had she said something wrong?

"Thanks, I will." She nodded more to herself than to Cassie, and once again reached out to cover her hand. "I was so worried you would be upset or think I'm a fool. I should have known better. You have a big heart."

"I would never think you're a fool, Mom. You deserve to be happy." Cassie couldn't help fixating on the last thing her mom had said. *You have a big heart.* She used to. But it had gotten her into trouble. And since then, it had shrunk.

She was glad her mother still seemed to think otherwise. But then, she didn't know about James. No one did. And Cassie had no plans to tell anyone about that time of her life. No plans at all.

Chapter Three

The more he thought about it, the more he tried to convince himself that asking Cassie for business help wasn't a good idea. Austin had been solely responsible for making the ranch's decisions for over a decade, ever since he and Randy hammered out an arrangement about their inheritance. If Austin was on the fence about something, he'd ask his brother for his opinion. Bo Nichol, his right-hand man, weighed in from time to time, too. But advice on how to actually run the ranch?

He didn't need that.

He didn't want it, either.

But he didn't really have a choice if he wanted her to stay.

Austin strode past the stables Monday afternoon. He'd finished all the pressing ranch work and had just brushed down his horse, Jupiter, before returning him to the pasture. Now if he could just get this conversation with Cassie over with, maybe the jittery feeling thrumming in his veins would stop, and he could get back to his normal tasks. Although, admittedly, those filled him with dread, too.

This was all their fault—his friends. The whole lot of them had talked him into this. Why had he even listened to them? He should ignore the advice they'd pelted him with Saturday night. And he should forget he'd agreed to go along with their plans.

He strode into the barn and headed straight to his office. It smelled like stale coffee, gas fumes from the UTV in the bay and, yep, there was the whiff of manure. The aromas of ranch life.

He took a seat in his office chair. It was only slightly broken. The back tended to fall off if he leaned back too far, and he'd duct-taped the right arm together more than once. From the squeak of the wheels, he supposed it was time to get out the WD-40 again. Not now, though.

After opening the top drawer, he took the ledger book out from under a manila folder containing the hay quotes. He'd talked to the farmer this morning, and they'd set up a delivery date. He and Sawyer were splitting the load. The hay would cost him a pretty penny, but it would also keep the cattle fed for a few months. It gave him a whisper of breathing room to figure out when and by how much he was reducing the herd.

Deep down, he knew he had to sell at least 15 percent. When all was said and done, it might be closer to 25 percent. Bile rose in his throat.

He couldn't do it. He couldn't sell them, knowing it would destroy next year's profits. But if he didn't sell, there would be *no* profits.

He wouldn't think about that now. He had another crisis to avert.

Cassie. Specifically, Cassie leaving.

He leaned back—not too far—in the chair with his hands behind his head. The delicate balance of his spine against the chair reminded him of the ranch. One shift too far, and it would all come crashing down.

This year was going to be a disaster.

And if he had to deal with disaster on the ranch front, he certainly couldn't handle dealing with it on the home front, too.

The guys were right. It was time to have a serious chat with Cassie.

He closed the book and stood, tucking it under his arm as he took long strides through the pole barn, out into the sunshine an hour earlier than he usually quit for the day.

What he was about to propose was way out of his comfort zone. He'd countered every reason the guys threw his way about their so-called operation. Every reason except one.

And that one was a biggie.

While they were organizing Operation Make Cassie Stay, he was organizing Stop Thinking About Cassie as an Attractive Woman.

She was the nanny. A friend. That was it.

He strode down the worn path toward the house. The grass was dryer than burnt toast. It crunched under his feet.

If the guys were correct, then Cassie might continue to babysit if she had more to do—like look over his books to see if there was any way he could make the ranch more profitable. It was worth a shot.

He hoped so, anyway.

Before he could talk himself out of it, he opened the side door to the house and quickly went through his routine of taking off his boots and washing his hands. Then he dried his forearms and hands thoroughly before girding himself and entering the kitchen.

Laughter and giggles came from the living room. He paused in the archway. Cassie and AJ were holding hands, swaying back and forth as she sang "Old MacDonald Had a Farm." They were on the pig verse, apparently, because AJ fell right on his tushy in a fit of laughter when he attempted to snort like Cassie.

"Did I miss the chicken verse?" He strode forward.

AJ spotted him, scrambled to his feet and ran into Austin's arms. "Dada!"

He caught him and held him up high. The boy's face turned even redder as he laughed and laughed. Austin set him back on his feet.

"You're early." With her head to the side, Cassie grinned. "How are the cattle today?"

"Good. They're good." He held up the ledger book. "Do you have a minute? I have a proposition for you."

Was it his imagination or did she blush?

"Sure." She turned to AJ. "Ready for our snack?"

"Nak!" He lifted his arms and bounced a few times for her to pick him up. She did and carried him to the kitchen.

"Here, can you hold him a minute while I get things ready?" Cassie handed AJ to Austin. "Milk and animal crackers. Do you want some, too?"

"Of course," he said. "I wouldn't turn those down."

"I'll pour yours into a real glass." She winked. "Only AJ gets the special sippy cup."

"Mine." AJ pointed to his little chest, his brown eyes big and serious as Austin carried him to the table.

"Don't worry, bud, I won't take your special cup." AJ wrapped his arms around Austin's neck and burrowed his cheek into his shoulder. Austin rubbed his back. "Getting tired, aren't you?"

"No!" His head popped up, and then he shook it. "No."

Austin met Cassie's gaze across the counter. She mouthed, *Yes*. He suppressed a chuckle.

A minute later, she set the sippy cup of milk, a glass for Austin and a plastic bowl with animal crackers in front of them. AJ was sitting on his lap, and the boy grabbed three crackers in one fist and clutched the sippy cup with the other. Cassie set her cup of tea down before taking a seat kitty-corner from them.

They all munched on the crackers for a few minutes, and he enjoyed the easy silence. After finishing the crackers, AJ grew heavier. By the time the sippy cup was empty, the child had fallen asleep.

"I'll go put him in his crib." Austin hitched his chin toward the staircase. "Be right back."

After going upstairs and carefully placing AJ in the crib, he kissed two fingers and lightly pressed them to the boy's forehead, then made his way back to the kitchen table. Cassie had refilled her tea.

"So what's this proposition?" She looked wary. He didn't blame her.

"You said you have a business degree."

She nodded.

"Well, I have a business problem." A thousand problems was more like it. To his surprise, the words were coming out much smoother than he'd anticipated. "I'm wondering if you would be willing to look over my books and give me some advice. Tell me what you think."

Okay, those words produced instant heartburn. What if she agreed to review everything and thought he was mismanaging the ranch?

He didn't have a college education. Frankly, he hadn't done all that well in high school. He'd learned everything about ranching from his father, and as time went on, from experience and his friends.

"Oh, I don't know." The quick shake of her head and shyness in her eyes surprised him. Cassie was always confident. She had no problem teasing him or setting him straight when it came to AJ. She stretched her neck, causing it to crack. "I don't know anything about ranching."

"But you do know about basic business."

"Well, yeah, but I don't have much experience. I mean, I was working retail for six months after I graduated, and I only had a few temp jobs in my actual field. Then Gramps got worse and…"

He hadn't known any of that. If she lacked experience…hmm…maybe he could offer her something she couldn't refuse.

"This would give you the experience you need. In fact, you can use me as a reference regarding your business skills if you want." He patted himself on the back for his quick thinking.

"Why?" She narrowed her eyes. "You never wanted my help before."

He swallowed hard. Honesty was the best policy, right?

"I don't want you to leave." He shrugged, meeting her eyes. "I'm hoping you'll stay."

"But not to help you with the ranch." She nonchalantly picked up her mug and took a sip. "You want me here for AJ."

"I know it's not enough for you." His voice was low. "Maybe this would tip the scales—maybe if you did both, it would be enough. I can give you a raise."

He wasn't sure how he'd afford it, but what choice did he have? Plus, there were assets he hadn't tapped into yet. From the minute he'd brought AJ home, he'd promised himself Camila's retirement fund and small life insurance policy would be set aside for AJ when he got older. The monthly survivor benefits paid for part of Cassie's salary. If he had to dip into Camila's life insurance payout to keep her, he would. The important thing was not losing her.

"Do you really want an outside opinion?" she asked.

He scratched the back of his neck. He didn't know. It had seemed like a reasonable plan at the time. He wasn't good at spinning things the way some people were.

"I'm out of options." As the words came out, he realized they were true. "And I'm afraid I'll cripple the ranch if I don't make the right decisions."

"Why me?" She narrowed her eyes with the mug resting between her fingers. "Why not ask your friends?"

"I told you. I'm selfish." He gave her a wry grin. "I need you to stay. AJ needs you. And only Sawyer really gets how tough things are for me right now. The other guys have a lot more acreage and investments to fall back on. I don't."

She stared into her mug like it would reveal the secrets of the universe. Maybe it would, and she'd share them with him. As the silence stretched, he fought the urge to tap his fingertips against his thighs.

It had taken a lot for him to ask for her help, considering he didn't want anyone judging him. She was probably going to tell him no, and then what?

He supposed he'd be right where he was now. With less than thirty days to find a new nanny, and precious time ticking by until the window to make decisions closed.

What would be worse—having Cassie agree or having her decline?

"I don't know." Those expressive brown eyes locked with his. "I'll have to think about it."

At least he was being honest with her. Cassie would give him that.

The last thing she thought she'd hear come out of Austin's mouth this afternoon was that he wanted her help—business help, anyway.

Of course, Austin being Austin, he'd told her the truth—this was a pitch to make her stay. She couldn't fault him for it. But she let out a small sigh, nonetheless.

She wished he'd asked her because he actually needed her business advice.

James had liked her because she'd been young and hung on his every word. He hadn't taken her seriously.

Austin wanted a nanny for his son. He didn't take her seriously, either.

A twinge of anger pricked her chest. She had a degree. She'd taken four years of classes on everything from economics and accounting to supply-chain management. She *was* qualified to give him advice about the ranch.

Nudging her chin in the air, she watched him. His jaw was firm, his posture straight, as if he'd take on anything life threw at him without flinching.

Then she noticed the glimmer in his eyes. Was it—no, it couldn't be. Could it? She squinted. Yes, he had a look of desperation about him.

Asking her—the nanny with a business degree—was his version of desperate?

It was all she could do not to shake her head in disgust and mutter, *Men.*

"No, I don't think I want to do that." She stood, pivoting to the counter where her things were. It would just be another round of dealing with a man she admired who pulled the strings in their relationship for his own ends.

Austin didn't need business help.

He needed a nanny.

And keeping her employed, even if it meant pretending to want her advice, was the path of least resistance for him.

"I thought you wanted to put your degree to use." He'd risen and followed her.

"Not like this." She reached over to gather her purse and tote bag. Tossed her phone into the purse and dug around for her keys.

"Like what?" The man had the nerve to look confused.

She set her purse back down and propped her hands on her hips. Then she realized how close they were. Only a few feet apart. Tempted to step back, create distance, she held her ground. *Don't give an inch on this. You know he'll take it.*

"Like…" She fumbled around for the right words and couldn't find them. "Like asking me for business advice is your last resort. You're throwing me a consolation prize. This feels fake."

"I'm not fake."

"I didn't say you were. But you asking me for business advice? That's fake." She jutted one hip out and watched his reaction. She and Austin had built a good relationship over the past year. He listened to her about AJ, and she appreciated his honesty. So having this conversation genuinely surprised her.

James pretended to need you, too. And you trusted him. And what about your dad? He acted like you were his whole world, and then he found a new family and deserted you like you never mattered to him at all.

A glint of challenge gleamed in his eyes. "Me asking you for business advice is not fake. But I'll admit my pride doesn't want to trust you with this."

"Because you think I won't make a difference."

"No, because I don't want *anyone* involved. It's not about you." He massaged the back of his neck. "Honestly, it's my stupid pride. I guess I don't want to be judged."

"Why would I judge you?"

"Forget it."

Was he worried she'd find a red flag in his books and call him out on it? She couldn't imagine him doing anything unethical or illegal. On Friday he'd mentioned not knowing how to feed the cattle amid rising costs. Maybe the ranch was in worse shape than he'd let on.

She might be able to see something he hadn't.

Oh, boy. She was actually considering doing this.

Before she could talk herself out of it, she figured she'd better get more information. "How much are you willing to share? In order for me to give you recommendations, I would need to review your books—income, expenses, how the ranch operates. All of it." She raised herself to her full height. He'd never agree to her terms.

"I know." The tension in his shoulders seemed to release as he met her eyes and nodded. His reaction surprised her. She'd been prepared for him to bristle and refuse. "It's bad, Cassie."

"How bad?"

"I don't know what to do." His jaw shifted, and he looked so lost all her indignation vanished. She wanted to reach up and cup his cheek with her hand and tell him it would be okay. They'd figure out what to do.

But there was no *they*.

"Why don't you tell me the basics, so I know what you're dealing with." She was going to need another cup of tea for this. And possibly a brownie. "Then I can make an informed decision."

"That's fair." He gave her a slow nod.

Maybe she *could* help.

And maybe she actually wanted to.

Cassie brushed past him, trying not to react to the feel of his strong arm grazing hers. He was a cowboy, her boss, and she was supposed to be showing him her professional side, not thinking of him as a man.

As she filled her mug with water from the tap, she came up with a list of questions she'd have to ask him. Then she popped the mug in the microwave and spun to lean against the counter.

Austin had filled a glass with iced tea and taken it over to the table. He sat in one of the chairs and gazed out the window at the sunny backyard. There was something vulnerable about him. He'd grown up in this house, was raising his son here, and he looked lost.

All the questions she had? She'd ask them. But in the end, she doubted she'd say no. Couldn't really.

Austin had given her a job when she needed one. And his little boy had brought joy to her heart during a difficult time in her life. AJ still brought her joy. Maybe too much. She was going to miss spending her days with the child. She loved being silly with him, playing make-believe with his toy farm, coloring pictures, snuggling together on the couch.

Whether Austin gave her a recommendation or not, she'd do her best to help him out. It was up to him if he wanted to take her advice.

No matter what, she was leaving at the end of the month. She couldn't settle for half a life, and it was all Austin could offer her.

Cassie was actually considering his proposition? It was more than he'd expected.

Austin wiped his palm down his cheek as he waited for the microwave to ding and for her to join him. Before long, she set the mug of tea on the table, then scraped the chair back and sat next to him.

She'd asked him for the basics. Basics. He had no idea where to start. Had no idea what she needed to know. His troubles blasted him one by one until his head ached.

"I assume this involves feeding the cattle. You mentioned it last week." She looked at him expectantly. Her words untangled his thoughts. *Feeding the cattle. Right.*

"Yes, feeding the cattle is my biggest concern." He felt calmer already. "The drought did a number on our hay production, and there won't be enough forage in the pastures for the cattle all winter. Sawyer and I are splitting a load of hay from a farmer in Ohio, but it's expensive."

"I take it the hay won't last through the winter."

"It won't last through the fall." He lightly rapped his knuckles on the table. "I have to sell some of my herd. I know I do. But selling them will cripple the ranch next year."

"Why do it, then?"

"I can't afford to feed them." Her soft smile encouraged him to continue. "I've always turned a profit." He leaned back, gazing once more out the window. The land was as familiar to him as his pinky finger. If he made poor choices, he could lose everything.

It was all he'd ever known. This land, this way of life, was his and he couldn't forfeit it. He just couldn't.

"Do you have any savings to tide you over?" she asked. "Could you take out a loan?"

The tug-of-war inside him ramped up. This was why he didn't want to involve her in his business. He'd have to bare it all. Show her the numbers. Confide intimate details of the ranch that he didn't want to share.

He studied her for a moment. Open, honest, intelligent. She was more than a nanny—he'd always known it. And he had no reason to doubt her business ability. She'd done nothing but bring him good since the minute she'd arrived.

He only had one chance at this or she'd shut down. And then he'd be stuck with a failing ranch and no one to care for his son.

She'd accused him of being fake. And she hadn't been wrong.

If he wasn't transparent now, she'd know. She'd leave at the end of the month. In all fairness, she'd likely be leaving at the end of the month regardless. He doubted anything would keep her here.

Yet, he desperately wanted to keep her here.

"I have some savings. It will pay expenses for a while," he said quietly. "I could take out a loan. But I won't borrow money unless I'm certain I can pay it back. Losing the ranch to the bank is not something I'm willing to risk."

"Makes sense." She pointed to the ledger book. "Is that where you keep all the ranch secrets?"

"I guess you could say that." He opened the book to the cattle stats and pushed it in front of her. Then he placed his finger on one of the columns. "This is how many cows I have. Down here are the bulls. You can see steers, heifers and all the other information on this page."

Soon he was explaining his rotation system for the pastures. Then he gave her a brief overview on the assortment of expenses. Cassie asked intelligent questions and took notes on her phone as they continued. By the time he told her the current price of cattle, over two hours had passed.

The sound of AJ crying forced him to his feet.

"Want me to get him?" Cassie asked, not looking up from the ledger book.

"No, I'll do it." His knees creaked as he headed to the living room and up the staircase. He didn't pause, just went straight to AJ's room, his heart melting at the sight of the boy standing in the crib with tears dripping down his face. A stuffed dog dangled from his hand.

"Dada." He lifted his arms, his face shining through the tears. And Austin picked him up, kissing both cheeks, and hugged him tightly. He couldn't remember what life had been like before he gained custody of the child. And he'd do it all over again—agree to raise the boy as his own—even if he'd known Camila would die young. He'd honor her memory by raising her son with all the love he could give.

"How are you, buddy? Did you have a nap?"

"No nap." His bottom lip swelled in a pout.

"How about some supper? You're probably hungry." Austin's stomach growled as if on cue. It was hard to believe he and Cassie had been talking for so long. Harder still to believe that instead of feeling like a failure or being judged, he felt relieved.

Her questions and the way she listened had taken a

weight off his chest. He actually liked telling her about the ranch. He wanted her opinion.

He gave AJ a quick diaper change before carrying him downstairs. Cassie had risen and was in the process of bringing her mug to the sink.

"Mama!" AJ twisted in his arms, and Austin let him down, frowning. Cassie was right about AJ thinking she was his mother. He wasn't sure what he could do about it, though.

She hoisted the boy into her arms as she grinned and pointed to herself. "Cassie."

"Mama." He wrapped his arms around her neck in an aggressive hug. Cassie glanced at Austin with pain and uncertainty in her eyes.

Maybe he was being selfish asking her to stay. It couldn't be easy with AJ so attached to her. But he couldn't stand to think of AJ not having her loving arms to run to every day.

Still holding the boy, Cassie met Austin's gaze. "I'll help you with the ranch."

He hadn't expected her to agree. As he soaked her in— her beauty, her tenderness with AJ, her vulnerability— he wanted to take it all back. Wanted to tell her the ranch would be fine and she should move on with her life, some- where bigger than Sunrise Bend.

Because having her stay would cost him more than he bargained for.

He wouldn't recover if he gave her his heart and lost her, too.

Yet, what choice did he have at this point? He was the one begging for her help. He'd flat out told her he wanted to change her mind about leaving.

"Are you sure?" he asked.

She nodded, uncertainty written all over her face.

"Okay. You'll have to tell me what you need from me."

"I will. Let me sleep on it first. We can talk tomorrow." Then she set AJ down, slung her purse over her shoulder and headed to the mudroom with Austin behind her. She glanced back at him. "Try not to worry. We'll come up with something."

We'll come up with something?

Apparently, they were a team now.

After they said goodbye, she walked out the door. He stared at it, shifting his jaw and groaning. He'd gotten himself into this. He'd just have to grit his teeth through it and hope for the best, whatever that might be.

Chapter Four

"I didn't realize you had so much land."

Austin kept the pace slow with Cassie riding Bonnet, an experienced quarter horse, next to him Tuesday afternoon. Her cowboy hat barely tamed the brown hair rippling in the wind down her back. She looked cute perched in the saddle. Her soft smile made his mouth go dry, and he couldn't seem to stop staring at the smattering of freckles on her nose.

Now that he'd shown her most of the ranch and explained how it worked, did she think he was making poor decisions? Had she noticed something obvious he'd missed?

"You'd be surprised at how many acres of land each cow needs around here." He forced his gaze forward again as they continued on the trail leading back to the stables. Cassie had dropped off AJ at Miss Patty's after lunch to allow Austin to give her the tour. Randy's mother-in-law, Patty Carr, was always looking out for them. They thought of Miss Patty as their surrogate mom.

"Really?" She gave him a sidelong glance. "Why?"

"Grazing. We supplement their feed for about six

months, and the rest of the time, they're foraging." The sun was warm but not too hot. He loved this time of year when the weather was mild. If he weren't dealing with so many problems, he'd make a bonfire after supper and look up at the stars. Thank the good Lord for his blessings like he used to.

"How much hay do you currently have on hand?" Cassie's question brought him back to the present.

"Not nearly enough. A month's worth, tops." Just saying it out loud soured his stomach. Every morning when he woke up, he closed his eyes and wished he could stay asleep. Forget his troubles for a few more hours.

"What other costs do you have besides the ones you showed me yesterday?"

He rattled off everything that came to mind. "It's a good thing I'll be selling the calves soon."

Too bad the profits wouldn't be enough.

"Have you dealt with these dry conditions before? You know, when your dad was alive?"

"A few times. None this bad, though."

"What did you—or he—do?"

He reached back in his memories as the clops of the horses on the hard ground continued. They'd been through dry conditions before; one year in particular had been bad. He must have been a freshman or sophomore in high school. Dad had been awfully quiet that summer.

"Now that I think of it, I remember Dad selling more cows than usual. And all winter he worked in town a few nights a week."

"Where did he work?"

"I honestly don't know. He told us he was helping repair tractors for a friend. I didn't think much about it."

She nodded, looking at the outbuildings in the distance. "A side job. More income."

A side job.

More income.

It should have brought him hope; however, the thought of an additional job only made his stomach curdle even more. He barely had time to do everything as it was. How could he possibly work another job, too? And who would watch AJ if he did?

"It's an option, at least." She smiled at him, and he briefly forgot his troubles. "Something to keep in your back pocket, just in case."

They continued discussing the upcoming expenses all the way back to the stables, where they took their time brushing the horses. Then they turned them out to the paddock and retreated to the ranch office. He gestured for her to sit on one of the stools at the counter lining the length of one wall. Shelves above it held books and binders.

Austin was acutely aware of how feminine she was sitting next to him. He spread out his quarterly reports. None of them were fancy. Just handwritten ledgers and notes.

The scent of her skin reminded him of coconut and vanilla, and he scooted his stool away a few inches before he did something stupid like lean in and accidentally brush her arm.

"Wow, this is impressive." Cassie pushed her hair behind her ear as she leafed through everything. "You did all this by hand?"

"I do every year. It helps me compare."

"You have previous years like this?" Her big eyes sparkled with eagerness.

"Yeah, up here." He reached up to the shelf above, selected two accordion-style folders and set them on the counter next to her. "Sorry, it's not exactly modern."

"There's something to be said for physical records." She unclasped one of the folders and peeked inside. "Digital data has its own headaches."

"Digital anything gives me a headache." He wanted to describe each paper she pulled out, but he refrained. Just sat there flexing his fingers, hoping she could make sense of his record-keeping.

Cassie scanned the first stack of papers slowly, then moved on to the next section and the next before swiveling to him, bumping his knee in the process. "Would you mind if I took these home? I'd like to enter all of this data into a spreadsheet. The program can run the numbers and come up with graphs and charts. They'll show the exact percentages for each year, and maybe we'll realize something we overlooked."

Spreadsheet? His mind locked down. Graphs and programs were not words he used often. "Uh, sure."

"Thanks. I think five years should be enough."

"You're going to type five years of my chicken scratch into a computer program?" He couldn't comprehend why anyone would willingly do that.

Her laugh tinkled through the small space. "You have neat handwriting. Once I set up the formulas, the whole thing will be a breeze. It's just a matter of typing in the numbers. You'll see."

"I trust you. But I don't want you spending hours on this."

She tilted her head. "I want to spend hours on this. It gives me something useful to do."

"Everything you do is useful to me." Heat blasted his cheeks. Why had he admitted that?

Her expression softened, and she packed all the papers back into the folders the way she'd found them. Then she covered his hand with hers. His skin tingled from her touch.

"Thank you," she said. "I needed to hear that."

"It's the truth." His voice was rougher than the rocky path they'd been on earlier. "Now that you've seen the ranch, is anything sticking out, you know, to fix my situation?"

With her elbow on the counter, her cheek rested on her palm. "No, not really. From what you've told me, you've done everything you could. I wish something obvious was jumping out, but it isn't."

He, too, wished she'd seen something he could fix. Then maybe he wouldn't wake up at night in a cold sweat. He'd take care of the problem. Life would return to normal.

Too bad it didn't work that way.

"I'll take these folders home. Maybe once the numbers are in a spreadsheet, a chart will reveal a solution. Oh, and by the way, I've started a list of potential nannies."

Austin had a flashback to the previous summer when Hannah, Randy's wife, had said those exact same words about starting a list of potential nannies.

Hannah had brought him Cassie.

And he didn't want to lose her. He really didn't want another nanny. Sure, Cassie seemed enthusiastic about making spreadsheets, but he wasn't foolish enough to believe it would make a difference in changing her mind.

What would change her mind?

Nothing. He had nothing to offer her. Nothing would keep her here. But he couldn't help wishing she'd stay.

"How would you set up a spreadsheet to compare feed purchases for a cattle ranch?" With her earbuds in, Cassie waited for Simone's response on the phone as she flipped through the piles of Austin's records. Where was the one she'd marked *Feed*? The Post-it note wasn't sticking out. She'd been sorting and categorizing his notes ever since she'd gotten home. But she'd hit a snag.

So she'd called her friend. Simone would know what to do. They'd been good friends during Cassie's final two years in college, and Simone now worked as a business analyst in Colorado Springs.

"What kind of feed?"

"Foraged grass, mineral blocks, that sort of thing." Cassie took another sip of the large iced coffee she'd picked up from Brewed Awakening before it closed for the evening. The ice had almost melted, but it still tasted delicious.

"It depends on your goals." Simone threw out several options.

"All of those. I'm thinking I need to incorporate weather conditions in there somehow, too."

"Weather? Why?"

"I didn't realize it affected a ranch so much." She'd enjoyed spending the afternoon on horseback with Austin. It had been a welcome change to discuss the workings of his ranch. She'd reveled in the way he treated her—like a peer he respected. "The dry conditions have severely depleted the grass and hay this year."

"Oh, I see." From her tone, Cassie had the feeling she not only saw but was coming up with something she hadn't thought of. "What if you create a separate tab for weather? Then you can highlight when the conditions are hot, dry or whatever."

"Yeah…" Seeing the possibilities, Cassie tapped her pen against the notebook she'd opened. "I like it."

"Add a column for notes, too. Remember how we had that ice storm in May a few years ago?"

"How could I forget? I slipped and fell. Nasty bruise. They should have called off exams, but they didn't."

Simone chuckled. "At least we were together. Lysa and Brandi, too."

Good memories. The four of them had spent a lot of time studying, laughing and sharing their hopes, dreams and fears together during the final two years of college. Cassie still talked to Lysa every few months, but she'd lost track of Brandi.

"Are you still babysitting?" Simone asked.

"Yes, until the end of the month. It's going to be so hard to say goodbye to AJ. He's the cutest thing. But… I'm moving. I need to get on with my life."

"So you *are* serious about coming back? This is great! We'll have fun—it will be like old times. And I'm sure you'll be glad to have a real job again. The kid might be cute, but changing diapers and listening to crying has to get old."

No more diapers or comforting AJ when he was crying. Her heart tugged at the thought. For over a year, she'd gladly wiped away every one of his tears. And soon someone else would be doing it.

Would AJ call the new nanny mama, too?

"Yeah, just like old times." She hoped she didn't sound as wistful as she felt. While she loved her college friends, there were some old times she'd prefer to bury forever. "Any word about companies hiring in your area?"

"My firm doesn't have any openings at the moment, but I'll give you the number of a recruiter I'm friends with. Colbin has contacts all over Colorado Springs. He'll find you something."

"Thank you." She jotted down the number Simone rattled off. They caught up for several more minutes before ending the call.

Cassie slumped back in the chair and surveyed the dining table covered with neat stacks of papers. The sheer amount of data was overwhelming. Plugging in all the numbers would be a big job.

At the end of the day, would any of it make a difference?

Dropping her head into her hands, she sighed. Austin had trusted her with the intimate details of his ranch. And the income and expenses didn't lie.

He was 100 percent correct. He did not—would not—have enough money to survive the next year.

Unless she came up with a solution, he would be forced to sell cattle and fire employees. Even that might not be enough.

Taking a deep breath, she straightened. There had to be something in here that would help him out. Austin had given her a job when she'd needed one. She'd find a way to help him, too.

Austin popped the last bite of toast into his mouth as Cassie walked in the next morning. AJ ran to her, yelling, "Mama!" After setting her purse and bag down, she laughed, hoisted him into her arms and kissed both of his chubby cheeks.

Then, giving the boy a big grin, she pointed to herself and said, "Cassie."

"Mama." He wrapped his arms around her neck and snuggled into her embrace.

Austin forgot to chew. They could easily be mother and child. The way Cassie's eyelids dropped softly as she shifted the boy to her hip told him everything he needed to know. She loved his kid as much as he did.

It wasn't new information, but it choked him up just the same.

Lunging for the mug of coffee on the counter next to where he stood, he hastily took a gulp. Yesterday had been necessary, but even so, he regretted it. Riding with Cassie all afternoon had only heightened his awareness of her. The questions she'd asked, the way she listened and observed while he spoke made him wonder why he hadn't taken her out on a tour of the ranch long ago.

It had been one of the best afternoons he'd had in years. There was something calming about being around Cassie. And the twinkle in her eyes made him feel young again. He hadn't felt young since he was twenty-one years old.

Yeah, and now you're old, especially compared to her. Don't forget it.

She set AJ back on his feet and took out a mug to pour herself a cup of coffee. "I enjoyed seeing the ranch yesterday. It's beautiful. Amazing, really."

She thought the ranch was amazing? He stood taller. "I enjoyed it, too."

Too much, in fact.

"Are you alright with me keeping your files the rest of the week?"

"Why?" He frowned.

"The spreadsheets I mentioned. There is a ton of data to type in. I'll be doing it in batches. You can keep everything I'm not currently using if that would help."

"How long are we talking about? I don't have a problem with you having the files, but I use the information in them often. I never know what I might need to look up."

"I understand. Um, give me a week."

"Uh," he rubbed the back of his neck, "like I said, I don't want you spending all your time coming up with charts and stuff. I don't know that I'd be able to use them much, anyhow."

From the hurt expression flitting across her face, he guessed he'd said the wrong thing.

"They might show a pattern we can't see," she said.

"What do you mean?" He leaned against the counter and took another drink of coffee.

"When you see everything displayed in a graph form, it might trigger an idea."

Maybe. He doubted it, though.

AJ launched into him, causing a few drops of coffee to slosh out of his mug. The kid attached himself to his leg like a burr on a dog.

"Dada, wide!" AJ held on to Austin's jeans and bounced. Every night after supper, Austin got on his hands and knees and let AJ ride him like a pony around the living room. The boy loved it so much he wanted to *wide* all the time.

"Later on, bud. My knees can't take it this early."

"Wide, wide!" Those little eyes brimmed with hope. Austin glanced at Cassie, who appeared on the verge of laughter, and shook his head. AJ then turned hopeful eyes to Cassie. "Mama, wide?"

"Oh, no. I don't think so, sweet thing. That's for your daddy."

He stuck out his bottom lip, crossed his arms and stamped his feet.

"I have something even better." Cassie went over to her tote and pulled out a coloring book. "Would you like to paint?"

Paint? Austin did not like the sound of that. Visions of the walls streaked red, green and purple swam through his brain. His fears must have shown on his face because Cassie nudged him with her elbow and gave him a cheeky grin.

"Don't worry. It's just water. See?" She held open a page, and he recognized it as one of those books with paint already in the picture. When water was applied, it became a watercolor painting.

Man, she was standing close to him. So close her hair swished against his arm as she turned toward the sink to fill a plastic tumbler with water. Then she almost bumped into him as she rotated to take the cup to the table where AJ was attempting to climb into his booster seat.

That got Austin moving. He hustled over to the boy. "You have to wait for me or Cassie to lift you, bud."

"No, Dada." He drew his eyebrows together and shook his head vigorously. "Me."

"You could fall." Austin tried to give him a stern look and was pretty sure he failed miserably. The kid was fearless, adventurous and way too cute.

"No." And stubborn.

Austin got him settled into the booster and waited for Cassie to bring over the water and paintbrush. She tore out a few sheets and showed AJ how to brush on the page. His son wasn't coordinated enough to brush very well, and soon he abandoned it altogether. Instead, he dipped his fingers in the water and smeared it on the page.

Cassie met Austin's gaze and shrugged with her hands up. He smiled. This was why he liked having her around. She set boundaries for his son, but she adjusted her expectations, too.

He watched the two of them for a few moments before grudgingly reminding himself he couldn't stand around gawking all morning, as much as he was tempted to.

"So the big day's coming up, huh?" Cassie said.

"Big day?"

"Mac's wedding."

"Oh, right. Yeah, Saturday. Are you going?"

She nodded, but she didn't seem very enthusiastic about it.

"Good. Save me a dance." He instantly kicked himself. Why had he said that? "I'm the best man, and Kaylee's the maid of honor, so I'll have to dance with her first…" Kaylee was Mac's little sister, who worked at Bridget's coffee shop.

"She's kind of young for you," she teased.

And so are you. Why did he keep forgetting it?

"She must be sixteen by now," Cassie said. "I see her driving to the coffee shop."

"She is. I guess she and Bridget share the same birthday. Mac made a big deal of it, or I wouldn't know."

"Aww, that's nice. I wonder if things will change. I mean, Kaylee works for Bridget, and the three of them will be living together, too."

He hadn't really thought about it. "I'm sure they'll be fine."

"You're right. Whenever I go into the coffee shop and they're both there, I can tell they really care about each other."

"Oh, no!" AJ yelled. "Mama!"

They both turned to him. The water had spilled and was running off the edge of the table. Austin met Cassie's eyes, and they both burst out laughing, even though it wasn't funny.

"I'll get the paper towels." He jogged to the sink and grabbed the roll from the cupboard below. Then he tossed it to Cassie, who easily caught it.

"I can handle this." Her eyes twinkled. She tore off several pieces and mopped up the water. "You go take care of the cows."

"I will." He glanced back one more time. "And don't forget to save me that dance."

Chapter Five

Weddings should be fun, but they only made her melancholy.

Cassie eyed the cake table and briefly contemplated getting a second piece. She'd tried the white-chocolate-raspberry earlier. Delicious. Would it be wrong to go in for a slice of chocolate?

If she hadn't promised Austin a dance, she would have left twenty minutes ago. He probably hadn't even meant it. It had been something to say, like, *give me a call when you get settled* or *let's get coffee sometime*.

At least she didn't have to make awkward conversation anymore. Only two people remained at her table, and they were related to each other so they had a lot to catch up on. She adjusted the top of her dress—a coral strapless number that flared at the waist and fell just below her knees. Her high-heeled sandals were surprisingly comfortable, but then they hadn't seen much action over here in the corner.

For the seventieth time—give or take—she took in the reception venue. Mac's pole barn was swanky for Wyoming on a normal day, but for his wedding, it was spectacular. Decorators had decked it out with string after string of lights. White tablecloths covered round tables, and bouquets of white roses were placed in the center of each. The effect was elegant. Beautiful. And his bride, Bridget, was, too.

If Cassie were to ever get married—which was doubtful at this point—she'd want a dress as simple as Bridget's. A church wedding. A small reception. Bouquets of pale pink flowers...

The DJ announced the first dance, and Cassie's gaze strayed to Austin. He sat at the head table, laughing at something Sawyer said to him. He looked like a model in that tux, but she still preferred him in his buttondown shirts, jeans and chaps. Either way, he was a finelooking man.

And her boss. She shouldn't be drooling over him.

She'd spent the past three nights typing in data and creating spreadsheets. She still had two more to make. When she'd shown Austin the first one, he'd been impressed, but she could tell he'd also been disappointed it hadn't turned up anything to help his ranch. Admittedly, she'd been disappointed, too.

Tapping her toe, she wished she could go back home and continue typing in the data. The house was empty since Mom and Carlos were on a date. This morning her mother had introduced her to Carlos. He'd been warm and friendly and easy to talk to. She could see why her mom liked him. The three of them had decided to go out to lunch next Saturday.

Another song came and went, and the festive mood escalated while hers tumbled to the floor.

She might as well just leave. Austin was busy, and she'd read into things and...

"Hey, are you ready for that dance?"

Her heartbeat tapped faster than a four-year-old in brand-new tap shoes as she looked into Austin's shimmering eyes. He held his hand out to her. She placed her palm in his, her breath hitching at the feel of his calloused hand. The lights had dimmed, and when she stood, he tucked her arm in his and led her to the dance floor where several couples were slow dancing.

When they found a spot, he put one hand on her waist and the other in her hand, keeping a respectful distance she found herself wanting to close. Who knew Austin was such a good dancer?

Everything about him, from his freshly shaven face to the perfect fit of his tux and the scent of his masculine cologne, appealed to her, and she caught herself letting out the teeniest, swooniest of sighs.

"Having fun?" His gaze bore into hers, making her feel like she was the only woman in the room.

"Yes?"

He chuckled. "Don't sound so excited."

"The cake was good." She tried to loosen up. "Jacey Sandstone was at my table."

"Oh." He grimaced. "Did she tell you about Rocko's condition?"

"Yes, I know more about the bulldog than I ever wanted to. I can't get the image of him drooling a path down her hallway out of my head."

Tossing his head back, he laughed. Her pulse took off at a sprint. She shouldn't be on the dance floor in this man's arms. It was too dangerous for a girl like her. One who latched on to mature men. She'd learned her lesson. Learned it well.

Austin would only break her heart.

And here she was—getting swept into her default romantic mode—again. The one where she falls for the guy who acts like he actually values her as a person, when all he really wants is a pretty face.

She needed to cool it with the doomsday thoughts. There was no need to waste a perfectly good dance with negativity.

Relaxing, she closed her eyes and swayed to the music. When the song ended, Austin led her off the dance floor.

"I should probably go." She blinked up at him.

"Already? Why not stay? I haven't had cake yet. Keep me company."

The only thing waiting for her at home was the spreadsheet she'd begun to create yesterday. "I *was* thinking the chocolate cake looks pretty good."

"See? You can't leave without trying it."

They ambled to the cake display and selected two slices, then brought them back to her table. The cousins were no longer there, leaving her and Austin alone.

"It seems all of your friends are married now." She watched him as she took a bite of the chocolate cake. "Oh, this is really good."

"Almost." He grinned. "Blaine and Sienna are the only ones left, and I have a feeling they'll get married by Christmas at the latest."

"What about you?" The words slipped out unbidden. She directed her attention to her plate, not sure how he'd respond. She didn't know why she'd asked it. Sure, she was curious about AJ's mother, but finding out his thoughts on marriage wasn't wise. She was already too invested in him and AJ.

"What about me?" He had the adorable clueless look he got when asked about something outside his expertise.

"Why aren't you married?" And she clearly wasn't able to keep her mouth shut.

His cheeks stained red, and he busied himself by polishing off the final bite of his cake. She should have known he wouldn't answer.

"It's not for me." His tight-lipped response only raised more questions. "I'm not getting married."

"Why not?"

He gave her the side-eye, and for once, she didn't care. Maybe she shouldn't be poking around, but she wanted answers. It was better to know the truth. Then she wouldn't be left with questions about AJ's mother.

"I don't know." He pushed the dessert plate toward the center of the table. "It's hard to explain."

"Does it have anything to do with AJ's mom?"

"No." He shook his head, confusion clouding his gray eyes. "Why would it have anything to do with her?"

How could he act like there'd been nothing between them? A pang of sadness for the boy's mother pierced her heart. Cassie knew what it was like to love someone, only to get tossed aside like her feelings had never mattered.

"I assumed you two cared about each other." She gauged his reaction, staring openly to try to understand.

"Oh." He seemed to go to a place inside him where no one could follow. "She's not the reason I'm not married. What about you?"

"Oh, no, you don't." She waggled her finger, trying to lighten the mood. "We were talking about *you*, not me."

He leaned closer, his eyes crinkling in the corners with amusement. "But I'd much rather talk about you."

Dangerous words. Did he have any idea how much she longed for his attention? Where had the private, gruff rancher she'd easily squashed her attraction to for the past year gone? This man, with his all-consuming gaze and those laughing eyes, wasn't making life easy on her.

"Well, I have firm rules about men," she said with mock seriousness. "And unless my criteria are met, I'm staying single."

"Rules, huh? Let's hear them." He leaned back in his chair, watching her intently.

"No. They're for me to know."

"And for me to find out?" His gaze held a challenge that sent the most delicious shiver across her skin. If he kept looking at her like that, she might go and do something stupid, like dance with him again.

Movement behind her chair had her glancing over her shoulder.

"Hey, is this where the party's at?" Randy and Hannah took the empty seats next to Austin. Cassie and Hannah had been friends in high school, and she adored the bubbly blonde.

"It is now," Austin said. "Did you try the cake?"

"He's already had three pieces." Hannah rolled her eyes. "I don't know where you pack it away, Randy."

"Yeah, well, someone has to." Randy took her hand and kissed it. Cassie suppressed a content sigh. So sweet. They were newlyweds, too, and she was happy they'd fallen for each other.

Sawyer and Tess joined them. He held out a chair for her, and she dropped into it, rubbing her swollen baby bump. "No more dancing for me."

"Good." Sawyer's relief was written all over his face.

Tess shot him an amused glare. "You're only saying that because you don't like to dance."

"True." He slung his arm over her shoulders and kissed her cheek.

Jet led his wife, Holly, to the table, and they claimed the two remaining seats.

"What are you all doing over here in the corner?" Holly asked.

"Just taking a break." Tess smiled. "Cassie, you're not really leaving us, are you?"

Cassie froze. All of Austin's friends had been welcoming and kind to her since she'd returned to Sunrise Bend. Time and again, they'd invited her to join them for their Friday get-togethers. And she'd turned down most of their invitations. Because of Gramps.

"I am leaving," Cassie said. "At the end of the month."

"Well, I think you should stay." Tess lifted her hand as if it settled the matter. "Bridget's apartment is available over Brewed Awakening. And I know Mac would give you a good deal on rent."

An apartment of her own. Above the coffee shop. The thought wrapped around her like a warm cardigan on a snowy day.

"Thanks," Cassie said. "I'll keep it in mind."

The ladies all began oohing and aahing over the wedding, and Cassie enjoyed listening to them talk over each other, interrupting and laughing as if it were the most natural thing in the world.

It reminded her of her college days. She missed her friends.

"Well, you have to join us Friday night." Hannah pointed to Cassie. "We're hosting. It's burgers and chips. Randy will get the cornhole boards set up. Don't worry, if it rains, we'll play games indoors."

The guys all groaned. Jet shook his head. "Forget it. If it rains, we're watching football. There has to be a college game on."

"On Friday night?" Hannah said. "College football is a Saturday thing."

Phones came out of pockets lickety-split, and the guys all scrolled through until Randy looked up. "TCU and Colorado. Eight o'clock, boys."

Tess and Hannah proceeded to argue with Jet and Randy about taking a night off football to play board games. Then Mac and Bridget approached, holding hands. Both looked happier than Cassie had ever seen them. Bridget positively glowed.

"Come on, guys," Mac said, urging them to join him. "Let's hit the dance floor. I've got 'September' by Earth, Wind, and Fire coming up."

Everyone got to their feet, and each couple headed to the dance floor. Once again, Austin held his hand out to Cassie, and once more, she took it.

She probably should have left earlier while she'd had the chance. Because the more time she spent with Austin and his friends, the more they made her want to stick around and scrap her plans for her future.

Around eleven that night, the dance floor still held a few stragglers. Most of the guests had left. Austin could sense the evening winding down.

All night, he'd been drawn to Cassie. Dancing with her had only heightened his attraction to her, and seeing her interact with all his friends drew home the fact she fit in with them perfectly. But fitting in with his friends wasn't going to keep her here.

He wanted Cassie to stay—for AJ's sake, of course—but if she did, how would Austin deal with these inconvenient feelings?

Cassie would never be content just being AJ's nanny.

And Austin wasn't even sure he could continue their easy relationship of employer-employee. Something had changed this week, and it scared him, but it also drew him to her.

"I'm heading home." Cassie gathered her small purse. She looked as bright and fresh as a summer rose. As beautiful, too.

"I'll walk you out."

"That's okay. I'll be fine."

"I insist."

After saying goodbye to Mac and Bridget, they made their way to the entrance and stepped out into the balmy air. The dark sky held stars that flitted in and out of sight under patchy clouds. A breeze rustled the leaves in the trees. The anything-is-possible atmosphere wrapped around him, made him want to stay close to her, to take a chance, to let his guard down.

When they reached her vehicle, Cassie turned to him, and he held his breath, drinking in her sparkling eyes and pretty dress. He couldn't let her leave. Not yet.

"So those rules you mentioned earlier…" He shifted his weight to one foot, arms loosely crossed over his chest.

"What? Oh, those? Never mind."

Should he reveal more? Share some of the stuff he kept to himself?

Normally, he kept it all locked tight inside him. The mood from the wedding and hanging around Cassie all night had loosened his grip on his secrets, though.

"You asked about AJ's mother earlier." It always hurt to think about Camila, but he wanted to be open with Cassie. Maybe not share every detail right now, but he could tell her some of it. "We were friends. Good friends."

"I see." Her eyelashes dipped. He gently tipped her chin up with his finger and looked her in the eyes. Wanted her to see his sincerity.

"We never…that is…we didn't date. We weren't in love. Marriage was never on the table for us."

"Then how?" A crinkle formed above the bridge of her nose.

"It doesn't matter." He shook his head. He couldn't tell her the rest. Not now, anyway. Not ever, probably. "You're beautiful, Cassie."

Her big brown eyes blinked up at him, and he was surprised at the uncertainty within.

"I know this isn't fair." He stepped closer, sliding his hand around her waist. "I know you have to go. But I can't seem to walk away from you right now. Not without…" He sucked in a breath. "Tell me to leave. Tell me I'm being a fool."

She didn't say anything, though. Just stared at him, and the longing in her eyes matched his own. Slowly, he bent his head and pressed his lips to hers. Her hands crept up his chest, winding around his neck, and he tightened his hold on her, deepening the kiss.

She tasted as fresh as her personality, and he sensed the loneliness within her as gaping as his own. As she kissed him back, it felt right, like he'd been waiting for this moment since the day his father died and his life fell apart.

He broke away first. He had to be careful. This was Cassie. His friend. AJ's nanny. The woman who was spending her evenings crunching numbers to try to help his ranch. This brilliant, breathtaking woman could never be his. For a split second, he forgot why.

"Austin," she whispered.

Was she going to yell at him? Tell him he'd taken advantage of her? "Yes?"

"I needed that."

He hugged her, whispering into the hair near her ear, "I did, too."

"Good night." She opened the car door, and he held it for her as she lowered herself into the driver's seat.

"Be careful going home."

She smiled and nodded. Then he shut the door and stepped back, watching until she'd backed out and driven far enough for her taillights to fade.

What had he done?

He'd kissed Cassie.

There was no way they could go back to normal now.

He'd blame it on the wedding. The fact that all of his friends were married or engaged. It was just the loneliness of not having a partner the way they all did. Wasn't it?

Austin slowly made his way back to the reception.

Maybe it would be better for them both if Cassie did move. She'd get the job of her dreams and have the life she always wanted. And he wouldn't have to worry about losing his heart to her. Because if there was one thing he knew for sure, Cassie deserved to have a guy who wouldn't freeze in an emergency, who wouldn't be dreading the moment when he'd inevitably let her down.

She deserved a guy who was strong, one she could depend on in any situation.

He'd proven time and again he was not that man. He'd do about anything to prevent Cassie from learning it the hard way.

* * *

Had Austin just kissed her?

And had she really just kissed him back?

Cassie brought her fingers to her lips as she pressed the brakes near the end of Mac's long drive. Flicking her blinker on, she checked both ways and took a left to head home.

Out of habit, she kept an eye on the surrounding area. Deer, pronghorns and other wild animals crossed these roads regularly, and the last thing she needed was to hit one of them. As she drove, she fought the urge to touch her lips again.

It had been an amazing kiss. A surprise—a wonderful, awful surprise.

The last thing she needed was a romantic entanglement with her boss.

Her older boss.

The one who looked smashing in his tux, who danced like a dream and who listened to her like she mattered to him.

He'd told her she was beautiful.

He'd also said he and AJ's mother were just friends, that marriage had never been on the table between them.

She frowned. It didn't make sense. How could he have gotten her pregnant if he didn't love her? That didn't fit with the Austin she knew. But how well did she know him?

Friends didn't just happen to produce a baby.

She didn't know what had happened. It wasn't her concern, so why jump to conclusions?

Sensations swirled as her mind flitted about. The pressure of his lips on hers. His arms around her—manly and strong and tender all at once. It had been too long since she'd been kissed. And she'd never been kissed by a cowboy.

He may have spoiled her for life. After tonight, she didn't want to kiss anyone other than a cowboy. One cowboy, to be exact.

Oh, no. This isn't good. I'm already slipping into daydream mode, and I'm not an eighth grader doodling my first name next to my crush's last name anymore.

The ladies had mentioned Bridget's apartment. Cassie could see herself there. What would be better than living over her favorite coffee shop? And taking care of her favorite toddler? Living minutes away from her mother?

It wouldn't be like that, Cassie, and you know it.

If she stayed, she wouldn't have what she really wanted. She'd only be the nanny.

Tonight had been a fluke. And she couldn't lose sight of the fact that when she'd asked Austin about marriage, he hadn't responded with *I haven't met the right woman.* He'd flat out said he wasn't getting married.

Cassie wanted love and commitment and forever and a ring and a white dress and all the flowers and a celebration like tonight.

She *was* getting married. Someday. To someone.

And she'd better not forget what she wanted or she'd end up alone above the coffee shop, pining for a certain cowboy who didn't share the same feelings for her.

There was only one thing to do. Get moving with her plans.

She still hadn't called the recruiter Simone had recommended. Cassie would call Colbin first thing on Monday.

It was time to ramp up her job search. If she didn't, she might be tempted to do the unthinkable and stay in Sunrise Bend, where her dreams had no chance of coming true.

Chapter Six

Church was a good place to look for answers.

Austin was disappointed that Cassie wasn't here, but she might have gone to the early service. He'd been so keyed up last night it had taken him two hours to get to sleep. No early service for him. Halfway through the sermon, AJ had fallen asleep on Austin's lap.

The congregation listened attentively as the pastor preached. Only the murmur of people shifting in their seats and the occasional cough could be heard. Up front, the pastor focused on hope and trusting in God to work things out.

Honestly, the message made Austin squirm. It had been a while since he'd been hopeful, since he'd trusted God to work things out.

If he were being honest, he wasn't all that happy with God at the moment. When May came and went with only a few days of sprinkles, and then June offered up no rain, either, Austin had faced facts.

God wasn't listening to his prayers.

He thought back on all the prayers he'd tossed out over

the past six months. None of them were about hope or trust. They'd been prayers of desperation. Pleas for help.

And they hadn't been answered.

He shifted slightly, keeping a tight hold on AJ. Maybe he'd been wrong to tell God how to manage the weather. But didn't He care?

Austin's conscience smarted. Maybe he was being arrogant. Who was he to tell God how to work things out?

Deep down, he feared God would let him down. That the ranch would fail. That his life would be ruined.

And now Cassie had entered the mix. He'd been able to keep his attraction on a low simmer for months. But the wedding—the kiss—changed things.

He didn't really trust God with any of it—the weather, the ranch or Cassie, either.

What kind of faith was that?

He cringed. If Cassie hadn't announced she was quitting, he wouldn't have opened up to her about the ranch's problems. Wouldn't have asked for her help. Or asked her to save a dance for him.

And instead of being wise and steering clear of her at the wedding, he'd taken one look at her in that pretty pink dress and been filled with so much hope—the wrong kind of hope, the kind a man has when he's thinking about a future with a woman—that he'd danced with her and stayed by her side and laughed and talked and...

Kissed her.

What a dumb move.

Dumb, dumb, dumb.

"'Blessed is the man who trusteth in the Lord, and whose hope the Lord is...'" The pastor had quoted this exact verse from Jeremiah three times already. Austin wanted to toss his head back and groan. "'For he shall be as a tree planted by the waters, and that spreadeth out her roots by the river, and shall not see when heat cometh, but her leaf shall be green; and shall not be careful in the year of drought, neither shall cease from yielding fruit.'"

Drought? His ears perked up. What was this about drought?

"Do you trust God? Even with these terrible dry conditions? The land isn't the only thing that experiences drought. Our hearts grow dry with longing, too."

He ducked his chin, his chest tight. They did have terrible dry conditions. And his heart *was* dry with longing, too.

God, I'm sorry. I've been praying all wrong. I feel like everything's closing in on me. The drought. The ranch. Cassie. And I'm sorry for blaming You for it all.

"God's arm is not too short," the pastor said. "He's all powerful, all knowing, and He loves you. If you're facing a mountain, ask Him to help. He might move it, He might help you scale it, He might hold your hand to skirt around it, or He might direct you down another path. No matter what, you'll be in good hands."

I am facing a mountain, Lord. Maybe an entire mountain range. I feel helpless. I'm out of options. I don't know what to do. I want to trust You. I want the hope the pastor's talking about. God, I need some hope.

The congregation rose, and he carefully stood with AJ in his arms. The boy continued to sleep, his warm cheek lolling against Austin's shoulder. Soon they were sitting once more, and the opening chords of the final song began to play.

Cassie had asked about AJ's mother. He'd shared more with her than he'd told anyone besides Randy. It wasn't as if he hadn't fielded a billion questions about her over the past year. He'd become an expert at staying vague, not wanting anyone to know the truth about his relationship with her.

Except he found that now he kind of wanted to share the truth about her with Cassie. Could he tell her the shameful details of how they'd met?

Not ready to answer that particular question, he sang along with the rest of the congregation. As soon as the service ended, he gathered AJ and the diaper bag and waited for the usher to dismiss them.

Well, God, if I'm supposed to tell Cassie about Camila, lead me to the right time and give me the right words. And if I'm not supposed to tell her, help me keep my mouth shut.

And on that note, he left.

Was her idea too out there for a rancher like Austin to consider?

Monday afternoon Cassie nibbled on her fingernail as steam curled from her mug of hot tea. She waited in her usual spot—the stool at the counter—for Austin to come in from his ranch work. The printouts she'd brought were inches from her mug.

She was fairly certain Austin would be happy about the hay sources she'd located. But the article she'd printed out? She didn't know how he'd react.

The additional data she'd entered into the spreadsheets was now transformed into graphs and charts. She still had more numbers to enter into a different spreadsheet, but it was a start.

Sadly, the numbers didn't lie. His financial position was precarious. He had to try something different this year.

The sound of the mudroom door opening brought flutters to her tummy. She slowed her breathing as the faucet ran, then turned off. Austin appeared in the doorway, and all the memories she'd been suppressing from the wedding hit her full force.

The attraction in his eyes. The way his palm had felt when she'd taken his hand. Dancing with him. Talking. Laughing. And then…the kiss.

"Everything okay?" He poured himself a glass of water and stood at the counter across from where she sat.

"Yes." Her cheeks warmed as she nodded. Was he going to say anything about the kiss? Had their relationship changed? Or was that wishful thinking?

"The wedding…" Deep grooves formed in his forehead. He wasn't going to apologize for kissing her, was he? "I had a good time. Did you?"

His nervous eyes searched hers, and she couldn't form a single word. So she nodded. And he did, too.

"I found hay for you," she blurted. She wasn't sure why talking about the wedding made her so jumpy, but it did. Better for her peace of mind to change the subject.

The way his face brightened chased away her embarrassment. She handed him the papers she'd printed out yesterday with the contact information for the farms. He glanced at her with a grateful smile and read the sheets.

"This is fantastic. How did you find them all?" He flipped through to the back page. "These all appear to have high-quality hay. I've been searching far and wide and haven't heard of any of these farms."

His compliment boosted her ego, and her back straightened with pride. "I did a specialized search using the hay analysis from two years ago, when the calves weighed the most at selling time. I figured the mineral content must have made a difference. There, buried several pages down in the search results, were the farms advertising the type of hay you need."

"This is amazing, Cassie." He handed the paper back to her. "But I'm worried I won't be able to afford it."

"Yeah, I worried about that, too, and I know buying it won't solve all your problems." She snuck a peek at the other papers—the ones she worried he'd take offense to. If he didn't like the idea, he didn't have to do it.

But she wanted him to like it. Wanted him to praise her for her out-of-the-box thinking. "I took the liberty of researching what other ranchers are doing because of the drought."

His eyes gleamed more periwinkle than gray in this light. "What did you find?"

"I came across an interesting article about a rancher who studied the profitability of each step of the meat chain, and he decided to keep a number of steers, butcher them, freeze the meat and sell it himself." She took out the article and slid it his way.

Austin lightly rubbed the scruff on his chin as he got a faraway look in his eyes. "I never thought of that."

Maybe he'd be more receptive to the idea than she thought. "He expects three to four times more profits this way."

His gaze snapped to hers. "Really?"

"Yeah." She nodded to the article. "On page three, there's a chart showing the average profits of the producers—ranchers like you—compared to distributors. I know it's kind of out there, but making the transition to distributing some of your own meat would bring in much-needed cash."

As he read for several minutes, she studied his face. His emotions were usually closed off, but she could easily tell what he was thinking by the time he reached the end. He'd gone from hope to skepticism to hopeful skepticism in a short time.

"I don't have the freezer space." He set the article on the counter. "And who would I sell the meat to?"

"He sells it at farmers' markets and has a small store on his ranch."

"Yeah, well, the farmer's market ends next month, and I don't have a store on my ranch. I see the possibilities, but I don't think it's feasible this late in the game."

"What if you took baby steps? You could keep five or six steers and sell the meat. It would bring in enough income to pay for the hay I showed you."

He seemed to consider it. Then he shook his head. "I don't know. I need to be practical. I don't have storage, and I don't have customers. No one's driving all the way out here for their meat. They just aren't."

Annoyance surged. She'd been right. He *was* going to dismiss her idea as unworkable. What had she expected? Him to be so ecstatic he'd pull her into his arms and thank her again and again?

This was Austin. Reserved, tough, stubborn Austin.

"Well, I tried." She gave him a wan smile, hoping he didn't see how much his rejection hurt. And why did it hurt so much? She'd known he wouldn't go for it. Was it because *she* suggested it? Or was it too odd for him to seriously consider? "I guess I'll take off."

She went to retrieve her purse and tote bag. Brushed past him as she set her mug in the sink.

"Wait." He reached out and lightly held her forearm. "The hay—the research—thank you."

Not trusting herself to speak, she nodded.

"Seriously, Cassie, I appreciate your help."

"You're welcome." As she looked into his eyes, she believed him. It didn't mean she'd helped much, though.

"Things were looking grim." He gazed beyond her out the kitchen window, then stared at her again. "They still are. But it's a relief to have more options, especially with the hay. I'll get in touch with the farms tomorrow."

Buying more hay was good and all, but making a bigger change, one that would actually make a difference? He clearly wasn't even considering it. She should accept it and leave, but the persistent part of her couldn't walk out without saying a few more things.

"The hay will help. But butchering the steers and selling the meat would bring in more money—a lot more than selling cattle to a feedlot would."

His expression clouded, and she pinpointed the moment he made his decision. "In theory."

She bristled. Hadn't he read the article? Why couldn't he see the obvious?

"Everything's a theory until you try it," she said softly.

"I'll think about it."

Yeah, right. She arched her eyebrows and turned away. He didn't fool her. He'd already thought about it and decided not to do it. That quickly. It had gone from *hey, here's a shot at saving my ranch* to *nope, too scary* in a split second. And it brought back memories, painful ones she wanted to forget.

Sure, Cassie, I'll be at the recital. I wouldn't miss it for the world. Dad. Eighth grade. But he had missed it because he'd recently started dating Sheila, and clearly Sheila had been more important to him than her.

You're being immature. Next semester, when you're no longer a student of mine, we can be more open about our relationship. James. Sophomore year of college. But she hadn't been immature. He'd continued to insist on sneaking around the following semester.

Was *I'll think about it* any different? It was still a guy patting her on the head who had no intention of following through.

"Look, you don't have to think about it. Throw the article away. It's your ranch." Cassie hauled her purse over her shoulder and gripped the tote in her hand. "See you tomorrow."

"It's not like that."

"Yes, it is." She held her head high. "It's exactly like that."

She was putting too much effort into Austin's problems and not enough into her own life.

"Cassie…"

She lifted her hand in a backward wave and strode out of the kitchen through the mudroom. As she exited into the sunshine, she tipped her face to the warm rays and trekked to her car. When she got in, she made a mental note to call the recruiter as soon as she got home.

A month ago, she'd decided to change her life. Find a job. Get an apartment. Spend time with friends. It was too late to back out now. And she didn't want to stay here. It would only hurt her.

Soon she was driving down the lonely two-lane road, absentmindedly noting the cattle to her right and the mountains in the distance to her left. She'd made this drive five days a week for well over a year, and for most of that time, she'd barely noticed her surroundings.

Her life had been predictable—get up, eat a quick breakfast and drive to the ranch to babysit AJ. She'd come home in the afternoon, chat with her mom for a while before she left for her shift, feed Gramps and settle him in his recliner to watch mindless television programs until he went to bed. Then she'd spend an hour or two scrolling through social media sites, listening to music or doing any of the thousand things she did to avoid thinking about her life before she fell asleep each night.

Until this summer. When Gramps died.

A burst of emotion clutched her throat. Gramps. Her hero. He had been so much more to her than just a grandfather. Gramps had been the dad her own father wasn't.

She eased her grip on the steering wheel. The previous year had been hard, harder than she'd allowed herself to acknowledge—to herself or anyone. Her beloved grandfather had become a shell of himself. He'd barely been able to talk and aged rapidly before her eyes.

The vascular dementia had taken his vibrant personality and left behind a confused, tired man unable to focus and unaware of his surroundings most of the time.

A tear slipped out of the corner of her eye, and she swiped it away. Then another one fell, and another, and she could no longer pretend she was holding it together.

He'd been gone almost two months, and she hadn't allowed herself to go there—to remember, to feel the loss, to acknowledge how much she missed him. The old him. The one who grinned and hugged her and bought her ice cream and acted like she was the only girl in the world who mattered.

She still remembered when he and her mom moved her into the dorm. Gramps had handed her a hundred-dollar bill and told her to buy something fun for her room. His big twinkly eyes had filled with tears as he'd given her one more hug before he and Mom drove back. She'd had to fight the big lump in her throat for over an hour after they left.

Maybe she wasn't only mourning his death. Maybe she was mourning more. The grandfather she knew and loved had been gone for a few years before he died. And she wanted those years back.

The stop sign leading to town came into view, and soon she was driving down Main Street. Instead of turning to go home, she continued straight, passing Big Buck Supermarket and the string of stores downtown. Finally, she parked in front of Brewed Awakening, got out and, shielding her eyes from the sun, stared up at the windows of the apartment above the shop.

Could she have the life she wanted here in Sunrise Bend?

She didn't think so.

After walking inside, she headed to the counter where Joe Schlock, the elderly man who worked for Bridget part-time and who had given her away at the wedding, tossed a dish towel over his shoulder. "Hello, Cassie. How's that baby doing? And how's your ma?"

"AJ is great. He's talking more every day." Which was good and bad, because he still called her mama, which only made her long to really be his mother. "And Mom's good, too."

"She and Carlos came in together the other day. They make a fine couple. It's nice to see her happy and smiling again."

She hadn't realized it, but her mother had been withdrawn and sad, too. For a long time. "I agree."

"What can I get you? The special is Maple Brown Sugar Latte. It being September and all, I figured it was high time we got the fall flavors in here. And since Bridget left me in charge while she's on her honeymoon, I'm trying out some new combinations. The Molasses

Mocha didn't go over well with Janie Lucas this morning. I may have added one too many pumps of the mocha…"

"The special—the maple one—sounds delicious." Molasses and mocha? Not so much.

"You got it." Joe continued to talk about coffee flavors and the high school football team and the new bleachers that had been installed, courtesy of Mac, over the summer and how they were much nicer than the flimsy old ones before handing her the coffee.

"Thanks, Joe." She tipped him and turned to leave. But she wasn't ready to go home. Couldn't face the new routine now that Gramps was gone.

Yes, she still talked to her mom for a while before her shift. However, after she went to work, the night loomed before her with no focus, no purpose.

No Gramps.

Just her. Alone.

Maybe that's why she was enjoying entering all of Austin's handwritten data into spreadsheets. It gave her something to do.

Cassie left the shop and began strolling down the sidewalk. The weather was still sunny but getting cooler. She might as well enjoy it while it lasted.

The Sassy Lasso had glittery orange and white pumpkins in the front window, along with leather purses and boots. Bound corn stalks stood on either side of the door of the insurance company. Everywhere she looked, autumn was being celebrated.

It was as if she was paying attention to the town for the first time in years. It was small. Charming. Home.

She checked both ways before crossing the street to the park with the pretty white gazebo.

Her phone chimed as she approached the structure.

With her coffee in one hand and her phone in the other, she checked the text message. It was a group text from Hannah, with Holly, Tess and Sienna as recipients, too.

Don't forget. Friday night is burger and game night at our house.

The urge to accept the invitation for once hit her hard. Why shouldn't she? She no longer had to stay home with her grandfather. And only a few weeks remained before she moved.

The loneliness of the past year caught up with her. She hadn't even known how lonely and down she'd been until recently.

Another text came through. This one was from Hannah only.

Cassie, please say you're coming Friday. It was so fun catching up with you at the wedding. Here's our address.

Cassie stared at the address. Owl Creek Road. A five-minute drive, tops.

The bench inside the gazebo called her name, and she took a seat, debating if she should go to Hannah's or not. It would mean being around Austin. All his friends provided a buffer, though. It wasn't like the two of them would sneak away for a kiss…although she wouldn't mind if they did.

Yes, she would. She'd mind. Because kisses only confused her.

No, the get-together was for burgers and friends and fun. Exactly what she needed. Without overthinking it, she texted Hannah that she was coming, then she responded in the group text that she'd bring brownies.

Feeling accomplished, she figured she might as well call the recruiter now, too. She found Colbin's contact info and pressed it. It rang several times before going to voice mail. After leaving a message, she leaned back and enjoyed her coffee.

She might not have it all together, but she was taking steps in the right direction. She'd get the life she craved. She just had to keep taking chances. It would all fall into place soon.

"Look!" Hannah shoved her phone in Austin's face Friday night as he stood next to Randy out back where they were grilling the burgers. "Barley made it through his first month of training to be a service dog!"

His thoughts in a jumble, Austin tried to rustle some enthusiasm as he peered at the picture. "It's hard to believe the full-grown golden retriever in the picture is the same rambunctious puppy you brought to my house every day when AJ was a baby."

"Tell me about it." Hannah had taken care of Barley for fourteen months as a puppy raiser. He was now working with a trainer to hopefully make the cut and become a service dog. "Those first weeks with Barley were rough. Remember how he constantly tried to lick AJ's face whenever he was sleeping in his carrier?"

Austin laughed. "How could I forget? He was obsessed with the baby." Hannah had come through for him big-time last June when he brought AJ home. She was the one who took care of his son while he recovered from a sprained ankle. Within a few weeks, Hannah helped him hire Cassie. He wished he weren't in a similar situation at the moment, needing full-time care for AJ. "I don't know what I would have done without you."

She blushed, then winked. "I don't know, either. You know I'm indispensable."

"Got that right." Randy sidled over to her and gave her a side hug. "You're one of a kind, Hannah."

"Right back at you." She kissed his cheek. Ned looked up from the grass where he lay and thumped his tail. Hannah grinned, pointing to the dog. "See, even Ned agrees."

Austin wanted to roll his eyes at all this affection, but secretly, he liked it. He was glad Randy had taken a chance and married her. His brother had the same heart condition that had killed their dad, but his love for Hannah had helped him overcome his fears of getting married. Although Randy could die or possibly pass his condition to their future children, they'd both agreed love was worth the risk.

Trust. Hope. Randy made it look easy. Meanwhile, Austin's fears kept swirling inside him whenever he tried to face the upcoming months. Every time he'd grown anxious this week, he'd think back on Sunday's sermon, and he'd say a short prayer for help.

He'd like to claim he had the trust and hope thing down, but he didn't. Not even close. There was too much uncertainty about Cassie, the ranch and who would take care of AJ after she left.

He might as well face it. He had to start actively looking for a full-time babysitter.

"Hannah, last year you pulled a nanny out of your hat for me." Austin rubbed his chin. "Do you happen to have another one in there? You know Cassie's moving, right?"

Randy pointed a spatula in his direction. "Hey, what did we talk about? Operation Make Cassie Stay is still on."

A fantasy, plain and simple. Austin had been foolish to think he could get her to stay. Even asking for her business advice wasn't enough. They hadn't talked much after she'd left Monday night, not that he blamed her. He just couldn't seem to break through the wall she'd put up. He didn't know how or whether he should even be attempting to break it down, anyhow. Their relationship was complicated enough.

"Well, it hasn't been working." A flame engulfed one of the burgers. Austin nodded to the grill. "Might want to flip that one."

Randy flipped the burger, nudging it away from the flame.

"I can't think of anyone off the top of my head, Austin." Hannah bit the corner of her lower lip. "I'll ask Mom and call some of the teachers. Someone might have a lead."

"Thanks."

The back patio door opened, and their friends poured out of the house onto the deck.

The party had arrived.

Cassie was the last person out, and Austin's chest expanded at the sight of her standing there in her jeans, T-shirt and athletic shoes. Her hair had been pulled back, making her look sporty and all too appealing.

He couldn't look away if he tried.

"Austin...earth to Austin...pass me the salt and pepper, would you?" Randy asked.

Austin swiped the shakers and thrust them into his brother's hand. Hannah was halfway up the deck's staircase to greet the ladies, and the guys were passing her on their way down.

Jet, Blaine and Sawyer formed a semicircle around Austin and Randy near the grill. They all joked about Mac and Bridget being on their honeymoon and discussed the latest weather conditions and the calves. Austin listened with half an ear as he continued to visually track Cassie, who was currently laughing at something Tess had said.

"I'm ready for the hay to arrive." Blaine cracked his knuckles. "That was a good find, Austin."

"Wasn't me," Austin said. "Cassie found it." On Tuesday, he'd called the farms to find out how much inventory they had and what it would cost to ship a truckload. Then Austin, Sawyer, Jet and Blaine had bargained with a farmer in Indiana to have a large shipment delivered.

As for Cassie's other idea—the one where he kept more steers and had them butchered to sell the meat directly—he'd shelved it for the moment. He wanted to discuss it with Randy. But not here. Not with everyone listening. Randy would probably think it was dumb, anyhow.

It was risky. Foolish, really, for him to consider doing things so differently.

But the numbers...the way Cassie had presented it... the article itself, which he'd read at least six times now— well, the idea kind of made sense.

"Where are the cornhole boards?" Jet asked, looking up at the blue sky. "There's no way I'm getting stuck playing Pictionary."

Sawyer shivered. "Me neither."

"There's no rain coming. Haven't had a drop in weeks."

Austin shook his head. "And if there was, we'd watch the football game, remember?"

Sawyer gave Jet and Blaine the side-eye, and even Randy had a sheepish air about him.

"Sienna and I are only staying for an hour," Blaine said. "She wants to get back to Madeline."

Austin almost rolled his eyes.

"Tess might be okay with watching football." Sawyer's doubtful expression didn't give Austin much hope. "But like you said, the weather's good. It won't be an issue."

His friends had all gone soft. Here they were, scheming on how to get out of board games when they could easily just watch college football. What had happened to them?

"I thought your wives liked football." Austin barely disguised his contempt.

"They do." Jet nodded, but his twitchy eyes said otherwise.

Randy pointed the tongs in the direction of the garage. "Cornhole boards are on the top shelf lining the wall next to my tool cabinet. Get the boards set up quick, boys."

Sawyer and Blaine took off at a run.

"Why the rush?" Austin asked.

"We all know watching the game isn't happening. And if we don't push playing cornhole, the women will get ideas. Bad ideas. I refuse to even think about Pictionary— or worse, charades."

A collective shudder went over them. The game of charades back in March had been brutal. They'd had a chili cook-off in Mac's pole barn on a snowy Friday night. Afterward, the ladies had insisted on charades. The women had loved acting out song titles and movies. The guys? Torture—prolonged and bloody—would have been preferable.

"Don't say that word around me." Jet, dead serious, shook his finger at Randy. "Don't even mention it."

"Well, then, they'd better get the boards set up right quick, because you and I both know what we're in for if you don't. Charades." Randy raised his eyebrows for emphasis. "Oh, and for insurance, tell Sawyer and Blaine to grab the ladder ball sets, too."

"When did you get ladder ball?" Austin asked as Jet sprinted in the direction of the garage.

"The day after the nightmare of charades. Ordered them online. Had a feeling we might need them."

Austin clapped his hand on Randy's shoulder. "You're a good man, bro."

"I try. These are about done. Would you grab the big platter for me? It's on the kitchen island. Hannah got it out earlier."

"Sure thing." With long strides, he headed up the deck stairs and through the sliding door, where female voices talked and laughed, making him want to back right up and retreat to the grill. He didn't mind talking to a woman one on one, but when they were in groups? Made him nervous.

"Hannah, Randy needs the platter." Austin weaved through the ladies, acutely aware of Cassie standing to the left of Holly. He nodded and flashed a brief smile to her, then continued to where Hannah lifted the white platter.

"Here you go." Hannah gave it to him. "Did he say they were done?"

"Yep." He avoided eye contact as he turned to leave.

Didn't want to get trapped in a conversation about whatever they were discussing.

"Oh, Cassie, can you take this down to Randy, too?" Hannah asked.

Austin groaned. He wanted to be near Cassie, but he also wanted to avoid her. And now his own sister-in-law was forcing them to be together. He didn't know if he should thank Hannah or be mad at her.

"Sure," Cassie said. A moment later, she held a plate of cheese slices covered in plastic wrap. He met her gaze as they crossed the deck. She shrugged. "I guess I'm the bearer of cheese."

"I can take it if you want. I have two hands." He reached out, but she kept a hold of it.

"That's okay. I got it."

They descended the steps in silence as Austin tried to figure out what to say. He didn't like this awkwardness, not when it had been easy—so easy—being around her for the past year.

"I'm glad you came tonight," he finally said.

"Me, too." The gold flecks in her eyes brightened, and he almost faltered. Everything about her heightened his senses.

And from that point on, he was lost. Didn't hear a thing while they all ate. Didn't pay a lick of attention to what they were saying. Didn't care if the women wanted to play charades or not. He was too busy enjoying Cassie.

Thankfully, after supper, they all teamed up to play ladder ball and cornhole. He was acutely aware of Cassie as his partner, the lilt in her laugh, the way her eyes twinkled whenever anyone started arguing over if the point counted or not, which they did often.

And when the night was over, all he wanted to do was

drive her home. Kiss her good-night. And convince her to never leave.

But when everyone said their goodbyes, all Austin could do was nod to her. Cassie told him she'd see him on Monday, and his heart sank.

He only had two more weeks with her, and then she'd be gone. Tonight would have to be a memory that lasted, because after she moved, life was going to be awfully lonely again.

Chapter Seven

It was silly to be nervous. It wasn't as if she hadn't met Carlos last weekend. And this was only lunch. They'd already made it through the getting-to-know-you-better small talk as well as ordered their food.

Cassie smiled at her mother, then at Carlos, both sitting across from her in the booth at the diner in Sunrise Bend. They looked happy. In fact, there was a shyness and joy surrounding them that reminded her of high school. She was *so* tempted to singsong *you've got a boyfriend* to her mother. She suppressed a giggle at the thought.

"I hear you're moving to Colorado soon." Carlos's brown eyes were warm and caring. "Did you find a place to live yet?"

"Not yet." She fidgeted. "I wanted to wait until I had a solid job lead."

"I'm sure a smart girl like you won't have any trouble finding a position. Stacy mentioned you have a business degree. That's impressive."

Cassie had a hard time thinking of her mother as Stacy. She'd always been and would always be Mom. Another thing she'd have to get used to.

"Thank you. I don't have much experience, though. It might take a while to find an employer willing to take a chance on me."

"You'll find something. Don't worry," he said. "Will you still move soon? Even without a job?"

Oh, boy. Here it comes. She'd told several people about her plans, and they'd been downright rude when she'd admitted she planned on moving regardless of whether she had a job or not. They thought she was making a mistake, and she thought… Well, she thought she was taking a leap of faith. That God would provide for her.

"I'm moving. No matter what." She kept her tone pleasant.

He nodded. "Taking a leap of faith."

"Yes, exactly." His comment burrowed inside her, affirmed her decision. She smiled at him. "Not everyone sees it that way."

"I know," he said. "I get it, though. I've had to take one or two of those myself over the years."

"Really?" Mom gave him a sideways glance.

"Yes. When Arabella and Thomas were young, I worked on a large ranch in Montana. But after their mother died, I knew I needed help. So I moved to Sheridan where my sister and brother-in-law lived. Found a job at the post office there, got the kids enrolled in school. Life was good. Hard, too, because I missed Lucy, but good because my sister's family became our family, you know?"

Cassie nodded, waiting for him to continue.

"A few years ago, Thomas and his cousin moved to Jackson to start their own auto repair shop, and Arabella got a good job in Montana. My sister and her husband moved closer to the boys. I realized I wanted something different, too. The smart thing would have been to move near one of my kids, but I prayed and found myself leaning in a different direction. One that didn't make sense to my loved ones."

Cassie listened with rapt attention. He was speaking her language.

"I have an aunt and two cousins who live in Sunrise Bend. That's how I ended up here." He covered her mother's hand with his own, squeezing it as he looked at her with affection. "Working the same shift as Stacy."

Was her mother blushing? Yes, she was. How cute was that?

"Sometimes you just know when you need to make a change, and sometimes you have to trust God will land you in the right place."

"I'm glad He landed you here." Mom continued to hold his hand.

"Me, too." He couldn't take his eyes off her.

Cassie took the moment to sip her iced tea. She trusted that God would land her in the right place. So why had she been putting off looking for apartments? If she was moving in a couple weeks, she'd need a place to live. What was she waiting for?

Her mind drifted to last night at Hannah and Randy's. How she and Austin had been paired together for the games. He'd stayed by her side throughout the evening. It had been easy to be with him.

The past two weeks had cooled her fire to get out of Sunrise Bend.

"How is the job search going, Cassie?" Carlos asked.

"The recruiter I called—Colbin—set up two phone interviews for next week. I was nervous about signing with his company, but so far, it seems to be yielding more leads than I've been able to find on my own."

"Are they both in the same area or in different towns?" he asked.

"Colorado Springs. Both of them." Which meant the obvious place to look for an apartment was Colorado Springs.

The cheerful windows above Brewed Awakening came to mind. Fridays with Austin and his friends…

"You need to call the apartment complexes. Don't wait too long." Her mom reached for her soft drink. "They might have wait lists."

"I know. I need to get on it." Their food arrived, and she waited for all their meals to be placed on the table before continuing. "I just wish Austin had a new nanny lined up for AJ. It bothers me to think I might leave him in the lurch."

"A nanny?" Carlos's face lit up. He turned to her mom. "What about Allison?"

"I forgot about Allison." Mom spread a paper napkin across her lap.

"Yes, she quit—what—six months ago? Pete said she's looking to bring in more income by babysitting."

"Allison?" Cassie couldn't picture anyone local by that name.

"Allison Jones." Her mom used her fork and knife to cut her chicken. "Pete's wife. She worked second shift with us. Pete works for the gas company. Nice guy."

"Oh, right." She knew them from church. They made a cute couple, and Allison was always smiling.

"She's a good mom, too." Her mother nodded. "You should have Austin call her. She's reliable and loving with kids. Plus, it will give AJ someone to play with as he gets older."

As he gets older... Cassie promptly lost her appetite. She was going to miss watching him grow. Miss pre-school and his first T-ball game and the first day of kin-dergarten and...she was going to miss it all. A wave of sadness hit her so hard, she had to bow her head as she focused all her attention on the grilled Reuben sandwich and fries on her plate.

"Want me to text her now?" Carlos asked. "I'm sure you and Austin want this situation wrapped up."

Her and Austin. If only they had more than a working relationship. They were friends, yes, but whatever was going on between them felt more complicated.

She was moving. Austin needed a nanny. If anything was complicated, it was her wishy-washy feelings, noth-ing more.

Holding a fry, she nodded. "Sure, Carlos, that would be a big help."

While he texted Allison, Cassie tried to ignore the heaviness weighing down her heart. She'd been excited to start a new life. But it wasn't exciting to think of Aus-tin and AJ starting a new one, too. One without her in it.

Really, Cassie? What about the job? The apartment? The friends?

It was all well and good to interview with compa-nies in Colorado, but would she be happy there? Really happy?

She was starting to realize how much Sunrise Bend had to offer.

"Allison already responded." Carlos set his phone on the table. "She's interested."

"Wonderful." Mom brought her hands up to her chest.

"Yes, wonderful." She hoped she sounded as enthusiastic as they did. Carlos might have provided the perfect solution for one of her problems. So why did she feel so sad?

She attacked her French fry. Austin didn't think much of her business ideas. And he wasn't getting married. He hadn't even married AJ's mother. He claimed they'd just been friends. Something told Cassie that AJ's mom had considered him more than a friend. How else to explain a *baby*?

She had to stop idealizing Austin. There was no future between them, and she'd better not fall into the trap of thinking there could be.

One heartbreak over the wrong guy had been enough for a lifetime. She was done pining for emotionally unavailable men.

"I think I'll start apartment hunting this afternoon." Picking up her sandwich, she smiled at her mother, then Carlos. "Thank you for reaching out to Allison. I'll get her information to Austin right away. The sooner he hires someone, the better."

"I want to run something by you." Austin glanced at Randy. They were playing with AJ on the front lawn of the ranch's farmhouse Saturday afternoon. The boy held a bubble wand and tried his hardest to blow gently but only succeeded at spitting at it and getting mad when no bubbles appeared.

"Oh, yeah? What is it?" Randy gently took the wand from AJ's hand and demonstrated again. The kid gave it another go. Blew too hard. Then he clenched his little hands into fists and looked about three seconds away from having a major meltdown. Randy crouched and touched his shoulder. "It's okay, buddy. You'll get it."

His lower lip jutted out, but he took the wand and gave it another try. A bubble started to appear, then popped.

"Cassie printed off an article, and it's got me thinking." And all the thinking was only convincing him that changing his business model would stress him out to the max. But he still couldn't get it out of his head.

"You? Thinking now? First time in, what, thirty years?" Randy laughed at his own joke.

"Ha ha. Real funny." Austin rolled his eyes.

"Here, buddy, try this." Randy dipped the wand into the bubble solution and slowly moved his arm back and forth through the air, causing bubbles to appear.

"Me, bubba!" Enchanted, AJ clapped. Randy handed him the wand, and he moved it back and forth, making his own bubbles. He squealed in delight.

"I'm in awe of your patience with him." Austin fondly watched AJ spinning in a slow circle with the wand in his hand. Bubbles drifted everywhere. The child giggled hysterically. Were the bubbles made of happy juice or something?

"It's easy to be patient with this little guy." Randy rose from his crouched position. "So what's this article about?"

Austin felt warm all of a sudden. Why hadn't he wadded up the printout and thrown it in the trash right after Cassie had given it to him? Why was he even bringing it up to his brother?

Because it just might work.

Or would it? Randy would tell him the truth—that it was too much of a hassle, too iffy, too much of a long shot. All the words he needed to hear.

Austin pushed back his cowboy hat to run the side of his finger along his hairline. "The decisions I make for this place affect you. They affect me. And they affect AJ." There. Good start. Now what? He hesitated. Best to just put it out there. "I've made no secret of the fact the ranch is struggling. With everything so dry and sparse, the additional hay I bought is welcome, but it's basically just patting a tissue against a gaping wound."

"I know." Randy nodded. "Don't worry. You'll know what to do. In fact, I can help you out with money—think of it as a loan—if need be."

"I'm not taking your money." Austin practically growled. "But I need to do something."

AJ was still spinning in circles with the bubbles. Not paying attention, he stumbled close to the tricycle nearby. Austin caught him by the arm, averting a tumble over the trike. "Hey there, sport, slow down."

"Bubba, Dada!" AJ grinned, his little nose scrunching.

"Yeah, I like those bubbles." He patted him on the head. "You're pretty good at that."

"What are your options?" Randy asked. "Besides selling off some of the herd."

"Well, I can sell off some of the herd or sell off some of the herd." He gave Randy a cockeyed smile. "Seriously, I'm going to have to. It's a matter of how many and when. But this article brought up another option."

Randy watched him expectantly. "Are you going to spit it out or not?"

He tipped his head back to the sky, sighed, then met his brother's gaze. "I could sell the beef direct." Just saying the words made his muscles tense. "I know, it doesn't make sense. I'm a cattle producer, not a distributor. I have no customer base. Nowhere to store everything. No clue what I'm doing. I don't even know the costs involved with butchering and packaging and freezing and…"

"Hey, back up, will you?" Randy thrust his hands out.

"How far?"

"To the beginning."

AJ ran back over to Randy. He held out the bubble solution for him to dunk the wand into. Soon he was waving his arm back and forth and laughing as bubbles appeared all over again.

"Basically, I would keep a number of steers to butcher throughout the winter. I'd store the packaged meat onsite and sell it directly to customers."

"What do you mean? Like the grocery store?"

"I don't know. The rancher in the article sold it at the farmer's market and at his onsite farm store."

"You've never sold anything at the farmer's market, and you don't have an onsite store."

Exactly. Relief swept over him. He didn't have to pursue this. Didn't have to invest in an idea that probably wouldn't work anyhow.

Didn't have to risk trying…and failing.

Randy tapped his finger against his chin. "What kind of income would it bring in?"

Feeling less edgy, Austin went over the numbers.

"That's a huge difference." His brother let out a low whistle.

"Yeah, but that's if everything falls into place perfectly. Like you said, I don't have a business or freezers or anything. I don't see how it would work. Plus, I'd still have to feed those steers, get them bulky before having them butchered."

"Do you have any other options?"

"Get a job. Sell some equipment. Take out a loan. Become a plasma donor."

"No one would want your cranky old blood." Randy grinned and fake-punched his arm.

"You got that right." Austin chuckled. "I don't know, man. I feel like I'm hurtling toward a cliff and running out of time."

"I'm sorry. I know this is hard on you. I'm serious about the money, though. We always have each other's backs. You'd do the same for me."

Austin got choked up. Randy did always have his back, and vice versa.

His brother scooped up AJ and tickled his belly, making the boy laugh and laugh. "Buy a few freezers. Butcher a few steers. Do a test run."

Austin blinked. Randy wasn't supposed to be getting on board with this. He was supposed to be telling him it would never work.

A vehicle kicked up dust coming down the driveway, and Austin's heartbeat hammered as he realized it was Cassie. What was she doing here on a Saturday afternoon?

After parking, she got out of the car and strode toward them. Her jeans, cowboy boots and lightweight sweater gave her an all-American look. His mouth went dry.

"Mama!" AJ sprinted to her, and she lifted him up to kiss him before settling him on her hip.

"Cassie." She pointed to her heart, then kissed her finger and tapped it to the tip of his nose. "Looks like you're having fun out here."

"Bubba!" He twisted in her arms and pointed to Randy's hand. "Bubba!"

"He's still getting the hang of it." Randy raised the

bubble container to her in greeting. "Why don't you show Cassie how you do it?"

AJ wriggled to get down, then squatted in the grass where he'd dropped the wand and ran back to Randy. He dipped the wand and turned in a circle with his arms out-stretched, giggling as the bubbles floated around him.

"Brilliant, AJ!" She clapped. He ran over and hugged her legs. She bent down and hugged him back. It did something funny to Austin's heart. Made him want to take a mental snapshot and tuck it inside to pull out later.

"Austin was just telling me about the article you gave him," Randy said.

Her pretty brown eyes filled with surprise. Austin fought the urge to shift to his other foot. He felt exposed.

"What do you think about it?" she asked Randy.

"Sounds intriguing. But I don't know the startup costs or what all it would entail."

"It wouldn't be too hard to find out." She stared at Austin with an expression he couldn't decipher. Did she think he was lazy for not doing the research? Or was she disappointed that he hadn't jumped headfirst into a busi-ness plan he knew next to nothing about?

Randy checked his phone. "I should get going. Han-nah's parents are having us over for supper."

"So you're saying I should expect a casserole and cookies later?" Austin teased. Miss Patty had been bring-ing over food and baked goods to the ranch for years.

"You know better than that. There *will* be food dropped off tonight. No question." Randy gave AJ a big hug, then said goodbye and headed to his truck, leav-ing Austin tongue-tied and awkward with Cassie only a few feet away.

"Want something to drink?" He hitched his thumb in the direction of the house.

"No thanks. I came by because I have a lead on a nanny."

A nanny. His heart sank. He'd forgotten about that. Wished he could forget about it forever. "Oh?"

"Don't sound so excited there, cowboy." Her eyes danced.

"You know how I feel. I want you to stay."

"It's Allison Jones. She has a six-month-old baby—a boy—and is looking to babysit to supplement their income."

"Allison Jones?" He drew his eyebrows together, trying to place her. "Kind of short? Big smile? Curly hair?"

"Yes. She's married to Pete. They go to our church."

"I don't know." He hooked his thumbs in the belt loops of his jeans.

"What's not to know?"

"AJ's used to having a lot of one-on-one time. Would he get as much attention if she's taking care of a baby, too?"

"Many kids have siblings. Sharing attention isn't the worst thing in the world. Besides, Allison seems really nurturing and nice."

"I guess I'll give her a call." He didn't want to, though. Why was it so hard to accept these changes?

He checked on AJ—picking grass from the looks of it—then turned back to Cassie.

He tried to come up with something to say. He should ask her how her job hunt was going. He should thank her for possibly finding a nanny. He should…

Beg her to stay.

It had only been one week since the wedding. One

week since he'd held her in his arms and kissed her. He hadn't stopped thinking about the kiss, either.

She tossed her head to keep the hair from blowing in her face. She was so beautiful and full of life. Full of dreams. Dreams that didn't include him or Sunrise Bend.

It would be selfish to make her stay here. She had big plans. And he wasn't going to be the one to keep her from them.

Chapter Eight

Cassie's foot bounced on the stool rail as she sipped her tea at the counter Monday afternoon. She'd finished the final spreadsheet, printed out graphs and even saved all her work on a flash drive for Austin to use in the future. However, inputting all the data hadn't coughed up any grand solutions for his ranch troubles.

At least Austin had talked to Randy about the article she'd given him. Maybe he'd even try it. She didn't understand why he wouldn't at least look into buying freezers and finding a butcher. And she also couldn't help taking his hesitation personally.

Had she missed something when she looked over the graphs? It was times like this she wished she had real experience in the business world. Her degree had given her tools and theories, but what she really needed was hands-on knowledge.

With another sip of Darjeeling, she let her thoughts scatter. Even with a good reference from Austin, she wasn't sure she'd be qualified to actually do a corporate job if she got hired. Doubts and nerves aside, she'd spent time researching the companies interviewing her on Wednesday. Thankfully, they were both phone interviews, which seemed to be standard practice for a first round.

She'd also contacted Miss Patty about babysitting AJ in the afternoon so she could do the interviews at home without any distractions. AJ loved Miss Patty. He'd be in good hands.

The side door opened, and Cassie stilled, listening as Austin went through his afternoon cleanup routine. When he appeared in the kitchen, she let out the smallest of sighs.

He was one handsome cowboy.

None of that. She glanced at the binder next to her and pulled back her shoulders. Her feelings for him would fade after she moved. This attraction was due to proximity, to loving his child—to thinking about his kiss...

"You can have these back," she said brightly. She patted the folders he'd lent her. Then she held up the binder she'd organized for him. "The spreadsheets and charts are in here. All labeled. Just flip through the tabs to find what you're looking for."

Rising, she slid the binder to the end of the counter. Austin opened it to the first page.

"You can see the breakdown in percentages here. And I graphed it out monthly so you can plan better for irregular expenses."

His gaze followed her finger as she told him about each spreadsheet and chart. Her confidence rose as he asked questions, and when she'd finished, she handed him a flash drive. "You can input the data yourself if you want. Then you'll always have up-to-date graphs and charts."

As their fingers touched, she couldn't help looking into his eyes, full of gratitude.

"Thanks, Cassie. I can't believe you did all this."

His praise warmed her. "It wasn't a big deal."

"It was. It *is* a big deal."

Their gazes locked, and the longing to stay right here in this moment hit her hard. She wasn't imagining his attraction to her, was she? It couldn't have only been the wedding atmosphere that had made him kiss her.

He was the first to look away. Then he coughed. "I called Allison. She's coming here on Friday for an interview. Would you mind being here to help me out?"

"Of course, I'll keep AJ occupied." Disappointment slithered through her veins. She was romanticizing again. "Or do you need me to stay later?"

"I meant with the interview itself. She's coming over around noon so she can meet AJ."

"Oh." Images of Allison playing with AJ, of him running into another woman's arms, pained her. "Yes, I'm fine with that. I'll be there."

"Good."

An awkward silence fell, and she didn't know what to say.

"Are you all set for the interviews?" he asked.

"Yes, Miss Patty is watching AJ Wednesday afternoon."

"Two companies, right?" His easy-breezy tone didn't fool her. His eyes gleamed with interest.

"Yes. For the moment." She'd applied online for several more jobs yesterday but hadn't heard back from any of them. Didn't expect to this soon. Colbin might have more prospects for her as the week went on.

"Like I said, list my name as a reference—a business

reference—if they need one." The low tone of his voice, the way his eyes gleamed, begged her to move closer, but she stayed where she was.

"Why don't I show you how to use the spreadsheets?" she asked. "Then you'll be able to input the numbers on your own when I'm gone."

He flipped the flash drive into the air and caught it. "I'll figure it out."

She leveled him with a long hard stare. He'd figure it out? Puh-lease. She knew him. He would stick that flash drive in a drawer and never give it a second look.

"It won't take long, Austin. This could really help you." She glanced around, realizing she had no idea where he kept his laptop. "Where's your computer?"

"It's not necessary."

"Look at me." She spread two fingers, pointing to his eyes, then to hers. "I'm showing you how to use the spreadsheets. Right now. Don't fight it."

He narrowed his eyes as his lips drew together in a thin line. Then he gave her a curt nod. "I'll get the laptop."

As he walked away, she pushed down the hurt his reaction caused. She should have known he wouldn't care about the spreadsheets and the charts. He liked writing everything down by hand. Doing things the way they'd always been done.

Why did she keep fooling herself that he'd appreciate her work? Hadn't he made it obvious he was only asking for her business help to keep her as a nanny?

I can give you so much more, Austin, if you'd just let me.

He didn't want the part of her that she considered

valuable. He wanted the part of her that made life easy for him.

And she'd been down that road before.

She wanted to be valued, treated as an equal, cherished. And Austin might not be capable of those things. No matter how much she wished otherwise.

Thirty minutes later, Austin's head reeled. Four times now, Cassie had shown him how to use the software and various spreadsheets and how to convert data into graphs. He still had no clue how to do any of it. Honestly, he couldn't even figure out how to open the program she was using.

Cassie wasn't just out of his league in the age and beauty department; she was out of his league in the smarts department, too.

"How did you know to do all this?" he asked, shutting the laptop before she made him find the program on his own…again. They sat next to each other at the kitchen table, and he was uncomfortably aware of the faint scent of her perfume. He should scoot away. Then he wouldn't do something stupid. Like touch her hand or…

"I learned it in college. And what I didn't know, I found out from my classmates. There's nothing like looming failure to motivate you." She pushed her chair back, angling it to face him.

"Looming failure, huh?" He doubted she'd ever faced failure. She was too resourceful, too plucky.

"Yeah." A faint smile lifted her lips. "I walked into my accounting class and almost ran out before the end of the first session. The professor was telling us to graph our homework, and I didn't even own the software she was using. The only thing keeping me from dropping the class was knowing it was required for my major."

"You didn't drop the class?" Her animation soothed him. She looked happy and bright…and impossibly tempting.

"No, I slogged through it. It helped that the library had drop-in study hours where tutors would help you with your homework. One of the guys was a year ahead of me and showed me the ins and outs of creating spreadsheets. It took several sessions, but eventually I got pretty good at it."

"I'd say." He gestured to the laptop. "This is way over my head. I think it would take me several weeks to learn all this, not several sessions."

"You're close, though." She placed her hand on his arm. His skin tingled at her touch. "You already know how to switch through the different files."

He didn't respond because if he told her the truth—that without her around, he had no idea how to get into the files—she'd insist on showing him *one more time*. He doubted it would make sense even after ten more times.

The past half an hour had convinced him to stick to his own way of record-keeping.

Besides, his method worked. He understood it. He was good at it. And he knew how to find anything based on what ledger the information was written in.

But he wouldn't tell Cassie all that. Not when she'd put in so much effort to modernize his records.

"If nothing else, I learned my way around a computer." She moved to stand. "Now that everything's done online, it's made my job search easier."

He couldn't imagine having to find a job online.

Couldn't imagine having to find a job at all. But…he might have to. A side job, anyway.

As Cassie turned to gather her things, he fought the urge to ask her to stay. But he had no reason to keep her here. In desperation, he landed on a topic he knew she'd be interested in. "By the way, I looked into the cost of buying freezers."

"Oh, yeah?" She glanced at him, her brown eyes shining with interest.

"It would require a large outlay of cash." He probably shouldn't have even mentioned it. It would only make her mad. "I can't swing it right now."

"If you had the funds, would you consider it?" Her voice was quiet. Warning prickles crept up his forearms.

Instead of being honest and telling her no, he waffled. "I might."

"Might," she said under her breath. "What do you have against it? Be honest. Is it because I suggested it?"

"You?" Why would she think that? "No. The idea… well…it doesn't make sense at this point."

"Why not?" Her chin rose a fraction.

"I told you. The freezers—I can't afford to buy enough of them. And we've been over the logistics. I don't have a customer base. I have no one to sell the meat to. It's…" He stood, facing her, and raked his hand through his hair. "I'm trying to give it a fair shake, Cassie. I am. But I have a lot of people and animals depending on me."

"I know, and that's why I think you shouldn't give up on it." She dropped her phone into her purse. "You say you're trying to give it a fair shake, but are you? Really?"

He bristled. What did she know about ranching? Why did she assume he'd blown it off? "Why is it so important to you?"

"Because you asked me for business advice, but you aren't willing to take it." She stepped forward to move past him, but this time he didn't just let her walk by. He reached out and took hold of her hand.

"I bought the hay. I appreciate you finding it. And all this—the spreadsheets and charts—I appreciate them. I do."

The disdain in her eyes cut him. Made him feel two feet tall. "Thanks."

The word hit him like a blow to the chest.

"I mean it. Why don't you believe me?" he asked.

She freed her hand. "Because you don't. Appreciate them."

"Yes, I do. Why would you say that?"

"Look, lie to yourself if you want, but don't lie to me. I know when someone thinks my ideas are good. And I know when someone is just patting me on the head to make me feel good. I'm not in preschool, Austin."

"No one said you were." He backed up a step. Preschool? Is that what she thought? *Fine.*

He wasn't going to stop her from leaving. If she didn't want to believe him, he couldn't force her to. It wasn't fair to accuse him of treating her like a child. He'd never treated her like one. He'd listened to her ideas. Had sat through this training session or whatever it was. He'd been respectful. Praised her.

"I'll see you tomorrow." She gave him a sad look and made her way through the kitchen to the mudroom. The door shut with a creak, and then the engine of her car rumbled.

He wasn't sure what she wanted from him. Doubted he could give it to her even if he knew what it was.

He wasn't cut out for big personal discussions with

anyone. He barely let his own brother in. He didn't even like to discuss his problems with his best friends. It made him feel vulnerable.

And vulnerability wasn't something he embraced. It could make him go to a dark place. He'd been in an emotional pit before, and if it weren't for AJ's mother, he'd most likely be dead.

Cassie leaving—being mad at him—was probably for the best.

So why was it so hard to have her upset with him?

He was getting too close to her.

He needed to let her go. For both their sakes.

"I'll text you the contact information for my apartment complex. You'll probably end up on a wait list, though."

Cassie was on the phone with Simone Wednesday night. She'd already thanked her for connecting her with Colbin. And she hadn't been surprised to learn that Simone had several leads for apartments, too. She'd done her own research yesterday, but none of the apartment complexes in her preferred area had any vacancies. Hence, this phone call.

"You can always crash on my couch for a few weeks if you can't find a place right away."

"Thanks, Simone." Gratitude dredged up emotions she hadn't felt in ages. She'd been relying on herself for so long she'd forgotten she had friends who were supportive and wanted to help. "I'll probably just stay with my mom until an apartment becomes available."

"Not if you get hired soon."

"True." But how soon would a company want her to start, even if she did get hired within the next few weeks?

"Just think about it. The offer stands." A shuffling

sound came through the line. "You didn't tell me how the interviews went."

"The first one was…meh. I don't think I impressed them. The lady interviewing me asked specific questions about my skills and goals that I'm just not in a place to answer at this point in my life. Plus, we didn't connect. You know how you get a vibe with someone? Ours wasn't a good one."

"Yeah, I do know and I'm sorry. I've had interviews like that, too. What about the other company?"

"They already set up a second interview—this one's a video meeting—on Tuesday."

"Way to go! What would you be doing?"

Cassie told her what the job would likely entail, and excitement grew as Simone told her about a friend who worked there and liked it.

"They'll probably want you to come out here for a final interview if they like you," Simone said. "You could always schedule some apartment tours at that time."

"I guess I'll find out."

They talked for a few more minutes before ending the call. She exhaled deeply at the thought of either flying or driving out to Colorado in the near future. Was she really doing this? Really starting over in another state? Far away from her mother and AJ? And… Austin?

His kiss at the wedding lingered in her mind, and she chastised herself for putting so much weight on it. It had been a romantic evening. They'd gotten caught up in the moment. Nothing more.

In real life, they had too much friction. Wanted different things.

So why couldn't she stop thinking about him? Why could she practically feel his strong arms around her?

Why could she see the glint in his eyes as he spun her around the dance floor?

Why was she thinking about the cowboy—her boss—as a man? Now? When she was on the cusp of getting her life together?

The neatly arranged stack of papers on the desk drew her attention. The research she'd printed out earlier. She slid the pile her way and debated what to do with it. Flipping through the sheets, a surge of pride hit her.

She'd located thirty-eight heavily discounted chest freezers with scratches or dents. On top of that, she'd printed the numbers of every butcher within thirty miles. All Austin would have to do was call and negotiate a price for them to process his cattle.

The bottom of the stack had several designs—logos, really—for Austin to print. He could use them in an online store, have labels made up, signs printed or whatever.

Would he appreciate her efforts? Should she even bother to show them to him?

He'd been dismissive of the plan from day one.

Cassie slid the papers into a purple folder, then moved it back to the corner of the desk. She'd gotten emotionally invested in his success. Too invested. Another week and a half and she'd be out of his life.

Maybe she'd be better off keeping her research to herself. Then she wouldn't be disappointed when he gave it a cursory glance and told her he wasn't buying freezers or keeping steers or any of the things that might actually save his ranch.

There was no point in giving him the folder.

She had her own life to figure out. And it was time to get to it.

Chapter Nine

❧

"Would you be available to work Monday through Friday?" Austin glanced at the hastily scribbled notes in his hand. Earlier, during his first cup of coffee, he'd come up with a few basic questions for Allison. So far, the interview was going well. The full-figured woman smiled a lot and seemed nurturing. Within five minutes of arriving, she'd hauled AJ onto her lap and handed him crayons and a few pieces of paper to scribble on. The kid seemed to like her.

"Yes. Whatever days you need me really, except Sunday. Pete always gets Sundays off. It's our family time."

"Understood." He peeked over at Cassie, who was sitting at the end of the kitchen table to his left. Then he turned his attention to Allison once more. "And your son is…how old again?"

"Six months." She beamed, bouncing AJ a few times. "Tyler's starting to scoot. He'll be crawling before I know it."

"AJ started crawling young, too." Cassie smiled. "You should have seen him. One minute he was rocking on all fours, the next he was into everything."

Allison laughed. "Babies. They seem to change and grow every minute."

"Do you think it will be a challenge for you to watch my very active toddler and your baby at the same time?" He held his knuckles to his chin as he gauged her reaction.

"No." She shook her head. "I've been babysitting most of my life, and I helped with my sister's kids all the time when they were young. I don't think it will be a problem at all."

He drew his eyebrows together slightly. He didn't doubt her. She seemed capable. So what was bothering him?

"AJ's used to having all the attention on him," he said.

"Well, it might be good for him to have a friend." Allison smoothed the hair from AJ's forehead as he ground the blue crayon into the paper in his zeal for coloring. "Keeps kids from thinking the whole world revolves around them."

His frown deepened. There was truth in the statement, sure, but… "AJ's already going to be facing a big adjustment after Cassie leaves. I want him to have all the attention and care he'll need."

"Oh, you don't have to worry about that." She waved off his worries. "I love children. He'll get all the attention he needs. Trust me."

AJ let go of the crayon and squirmed to get off Allison's lap. She helped him to his feet, and he went over to Cassie and started climbing the chair to get on hers. She boosted him up, settling him on her lap and kissing the top of his head. He tipped his head backward and grinned up at her, making her chuckle.

"What time would you need me to be here?" Allison asked. "If you hire me, that is."

"Cassie arrives at seven and leaves around three. Would that work for you?"

Her eyes grew round as her mouth spread into a smile. "That would be perfect. It would give me time to get home and put supper on before Pete gets off work."

"AJ always goes down for a nap at that time," Cassie said. "Do you want me to run his schedule by you?"

"Sure."

Austin watched the two women interact as Cassie filled Allison in on the day-to-day care. For the most part, the conversation went smoothly. He didn't see any reason why he shouldn't hire Allison—well, besides the fact she wasn't Cassie.

But he didn't want to hire her.

He didn't want AJ having to share the attention with her own son. Didn't want to have to get used to a new babysitter showing up every morning.

They wrapped up their discussion and turned to him expectantly.

"Do you have any questions for me?" he asked.

Allison asked if AJ had any allergies or health concerns. He didn't. Austin went over the pay, and she didn't have any objections. Then she asked when she would start if Austin hired her.

"October third." He glanced at Cassie, who held AJ a little tighter. "And if for some reason you can't come in—let's say you're sick or have an appointment or something—Mrs. Carr doesn't mind being AJ's backup sitter."

"Miss Patty is a gem, isn't she?" Allison said. "I still have two casseroles in the freezer from when Tyler was born."

He chuckled. "I probably have a few in the freezer myself."

They all stood. Cassie hoisted AJ onto her hip, and he laid his cheek on her shoulder.

"I'll give you a call next week and let you know my decision." Austin held out his hand to Allison. She shook it, and then he walked her to the door. "Let me know if you have any other questions or concerns."

"I will. I look forward to getting your call. Your son will be in good hands if you hire me." Then she gave him another bright smile, waved to Cassie, blew AJ a kiss and headed out onto the porch. Austin waited until she was halfway to her car before shutting the door and turning back to Cassie.

"Well? What do you think?" Tension coiled in his stomach, spreading up through his body.

"I think we should talk about it outside and enjoy this gorgeous weather before it's gone for the year." Cassie set AJ down. "Hey, bud, let's get your shoes on and go outside."

"Baw?" He clapped his hands.

"Sure. We can play with the ball." Cassie pointed him to the mudroom, and he ran with his heels kicking his behind.

"I guess he likes the idea." Austin shook his head, chuckling.

"He loves being outside. Winter is going to be rough." Cassie followed AJ and dug around in a bin for his sneakers. The boy had already found the blue-and-purple-swirly plastic ball Austin had picked up from the supermarket this summer. Cassie shook her head in amusement. "Hold on. We need to get your shoes on first."

As AJ sat on the floor and leaned back on his elbows, one foot in the air near Cassie, a bittersweet feeling pierced Austin. These days were numbered. The days of Cassie patting her lap where she sat on her knees, telling AJ, "I can't get a shoe on a foot dangling around in the air." Of AJ bouncing up to sit on her lap and wiggling while she got each shoe on for him. Of her helping him stand, patting his little behind in affection before uncurling her legs and standing, too.

He was going to miss all this far more than he ever could have imagined.

They made their way outside to the front yard where AJ threw the ball, watching it bounce twice in the dry yellowing grass before running after it.

"So, Allison…?" Austin asked as he joined Cassie to sit on one of the porch steps.

"Is great." Her bright smile almost met her eyes.

"But?"

"No buts." She shook her head, her brown hair swirling around her neck before she swished it over one shoulder. "She'll take good care of him."

"Good isn't enough." He stretched one leg out and leaned back on his elbow. AJ was still giggling as he threw the ball and chased after it again and again. At some point soon, the kid would wise up and want him or Cassie to throw it to him. Until then, he'd make the most of this time. "He reminds me of his mother."

Startled, Cassie looked at him. He pushed off his elbow and brought both feet to the step below.

"She, too, had a lot of energy and always had a positive attitude." He didn't know why he wanted to tell Cassie about Camila, but he did. Maybe he wanted her to know how important it was that he raise AJ right. "Camila had a bad home life. A rotten childhood."

Cassie's eyelids lowered slightly in concern as she shifted to face him better.

"Her mom died when she was young. Her dad raised her and her brother, but from what she told me, her childhood was chaotic, dangerous and abusive. The day after she turned eighteen, she joined the military. She had nerves of steel. A real adrenaline junkie. A bitty thing, too."

Cassie seemed to shrink next to him. He could imagine why. She probably thought he'd been in love with Camila or something, even though he'd already assured her they were only friends.

Yet, he couldn't shake the feeling Cassie deserved to know the truth. He trusted her, and he knew she wouldn't tell anyone around town and wouldn't hold it against him, either.

But the reason he and Camila met…

Shamed him.

Embarrassed him.

Was a constant reminder that he couldn't trust himself to be the man a woman needed him to be. Not if he couldn't protect a wife and kids the way they deserved.

And maybe that was exactly why he *was* telling Cassie the truth about Camila. It would cool whatever had been heating up between them all month. And that needed to be cooled. Badly. Plus, he wanted her to understand why raising AJ with love and stability was so important to him.

"We met when I was twenty-one," he said. "My dad had died—heart attack—a few months earlier, leaving me and Randy to figure out the ranch without him. I hired Bo Nichol, and two weeks later, I took off. Told my brother I was visiting an old friend. But I really drove to San Antonio, where our parents met."

"To pay your respects, so to speak?" She relaxed next to him.

"I don't know. I honestly don't know what I'd hoped to find when I was there." He didn't want to meet her eyes, but he did. "Nothing about that time was good. I was drowning in responsibilities. I felt helpless dealing with the funeral, the bank accounts, making all the decisions. Thankfully, Dad had trained me well. The ranch was the easy part."

She placed her hand on his knee, and he covered it with his hand briefly. Her support was appreciated, if not deserved.

"I'm going to tell you something only my brother knows." He stared straight at her, searching her eyes to make sure she knew he meant business. "I'm asking you not to share it. Ever."

Surprise flashed in her face, but she nodded.

"I didn't go to Texas for good reasons. I went because I was lost, and when I got there, I was ready to end it all. I got drunk—I'm talking all-day drunk. It was a little dive bar. I was miserable, hazy, and I didn't know what was going on around me. Some guys came in with guns. Camila saw me there and forced me to my feet, half dragging, half carrying me through the kitchen out the back door as shots were fired. She helped me into her car and drove me to her apartment, where I ended up passing out for a few hours."

As much as he didn't want to see her reaction, he forced himself to look. The scorn and disgust he expected to see weren't there. Only curiosity and compassion. Exactly what he should have known Cassie would feel.

Well, she wouldn't feel curious or compassionate for long. But he'd gotten this far. Dare he tell her everything? Every last awful, terrible thing?

Yes.

"I was in a dark place, Cassie. I'm talking dark." Her hand squeezed his arm slightly in a gesture for him to continue. "I'd turned my back on God. Considered ending my own life. Figured Bo could manage the ranch fine and that Randy would be better off without me."

"Why would you ever think that?"

"Because he found Dad's body, and it wrecked him. I'm older. I should have been the one to find Dad. It should have been me."

"You couldn't help it. It was out of your control."

"I know, but at the time, I was pretty messed up. I blamed myself. Wondered if I should have seen signs my dad was having health problems. But I couldn't think of any. If he'd had any symptoms, he'd kept them to himself."

AJ had stopped throwing the ball and was crouching and poking at a butterfly. It flew away promptly. Naturally, he began chasing it, then fell backward and sprang back up to chase it some more.

"Anyway, back at the apartment, I sobered up. Camila told me the guys who shot up the bar knew the owner and were there for revenge. I don't know all the details, but three people were shot. I would have been one of them if she hadn't gotten me out of there."

Cassie's other arm wound around his bicep, and she hugged it lightly. "I'm so sorry, Austin. How scary."

"It is scary. Scary to think that because of my dumb actions, she could have been killed. I never should have gotten drunk. I should have been aware of my surroundings. It should have been *me* helping *her* get to safety, not the other way around." His voice rose as he continued. "She was there looking for her brother. She told me I looked like a sheep without a shepherd, that she believed God sent her there to help me."

"Do you believe that?"

Did he? He thought for a second. "Yeah, I do. Maybe God was waking me up. I came home. Took over the ranch. And Camila and I became friends. Her brother, the one she'd been looking for, died not long after. Drug overdose. I'd go to Texas twice a year to spend a long weekend with her. She kept going up in rank in the military. And then she met a guy. In her own words, they got way too serious, way too fast. Within a short time, she was pregnant, but she didn't tell him because he'd started to remind her of her abusive father. He scared her, so she broke up with him, and he beat her up."

"That's terrible!"

"It is. She didn't deserve it. No woman does. No one deserves it, period." His jaw tightened, and he forced it to relax. "She called me. She was upset, and we talked it through. She was afraid he'd kill her and the baby if he ever found out it was his. I told her to put my name on the birth certificate. She resisted, said it would make me responsible if anything happened to her. I told her I would be responsible. She didn't have anyone else. No family. No close friends she trusted enough to name as guardian. I mean, she'd saved my life. The least I could do was assure her I'd raise her baby as my own in the event anything happened to her. I just never expected it would happen. Especially not so soon."

"AJ isn't your son." Cassie's eyes widened, then she blinked one, two, three times.

"He's my son in every way that counts."

"You know what I mean. He's not your biological baby."

"What does it matter?" He shrugged. "He's mine now."

"But you let everyone think…"

"What? That I knocked up a girl and didn't take responsibility until she was gone? I don't care what people think. I will protect AJ until the day I die. I will raise him as if he's my own. I love him like he is."

"Is that why you did it?" She stretched her legs out, crossing one slim ankle over the other. "You don't want the real father to find out."

He nodded. "Not that he would. He never knew she was pregnant. She got a restraining order against him, and she transferred to another base not long after. But if he got the itch to look into things, it wouldn't be difficult to follow a trail back here. Thankfully, the fact that my name is on the birth certificate gives me legal rights. I'm not about to throw those rights away by announcing I'm not his real dad."

Rubbing his eyes with one hand, AJ toddled toward them. Austin stood and picked him up, sitting down again with him on his lap. But he reached both arms for Cassie. "Mama."

Austin let out a small sigh. Like father, like son. Both longed for Cassie's touch. She made him feel seen, heard, understood.

Cassie hauled AJ onto her lap, and he reclined in her arms, one hand reaching up to twirl her hair in his fingers, and the other thumb popped into his mouth. Cassie caressed his hair as his eyelids drooped.

Austin's heart throbbed at the sight of the two of them. He didn't know what he'd do without her around. Allison taking care of AJ wouldn't be the same.

"How did she die?" The words caught him off guard. He shook his thoughts free.

"Brain aneurysm. She was working on base, active duty, and she collapsed. Even with medical care, she died within hours. Never regained consciousness."

They sat in silence, the heavy breathing of AJ asleep the only sound breaking up the wind and faint moos of the cattle.

Austin lurched to his feet, resting his forearm against the porch railing. "So now you see why it's so important for me to find the right nanny. I owe it to Camila to raise AJ with love and security."

"I do see." The way she said it made him think she meant something else entirely from what he was thinking. "AJ's a special boy, his mother was a special woman, and you're a special man."

He turned to face her. "I'm not special, Cassie. Don't think I'm anything I'm not."

"Oh, don't worry about that." She stared off in the distance with a solemn look on her face. "I work very hard at keeping my opinions grounded in reality."

"What does that mean?"

"You shared your secrets. I guess it's only fair I share mine."

Cassie cradled AJ in her arms as Austin took his seat next to her again. What he'd told her…she couldn't process it.

Too much to take in. Too unexpected. Too surprising.

But her heart was thumping with admiration for him, and one thing she knew was that when she did process what he'd revealed, it wouldn't be unexpected or surprising at all.

It was simply the kind of guy Austin was.

It hadn't escaped her notice he was hung up about his past. His father's death, for sure. The circumstances where he and Camila met, definitely. But she sensed more. Other reasons for him to withdraw into himself. To think less of himself.

She understood only too well how easy it was to withdraw, to think less of herself. Hadn't she been doing it for years?

"You don't have to tell me anything, Cassie." Austin's gray eyes gleamed.

"I want to." Did she, though? Her stomach clenched at the thought of putting her past into words. Where to begin? Where could she possibly start?

"It began with my dad." She held AJ's warm body, growing heavy with sleep, and it gave her strength. "He left us when I was eleven. By the time I was twelve, my parents were divorced. Gramps lived here, so Mom and I moved in with him for a while. Six months, maybe. I don't remember. All I knew was Dad lived an hour away, and I was crushed. I thought I'd be spending every other weekend with him. For a while I did. Mom got a job—the same one she has now—and we rented a house, which she later bought. And Dad remarried. Sheila had two small children. He stopped making the drive for my weekends with him. He moved his new family to Colorado."

"Is that why you're leaving? To spend more time with your dad?"

She hadn't considered the fact she'd be closer to her father. It was as if he didn't exist in her life anymore. Whether he lived next door or in another country, she doubted she'd see him.

"No," she said. "I'd barely started high school when he

stopped buying airline tickets for me to come visit. The calls trickled out. He forgot my birthdays and no longer sent gifts at Christmas."

It was Austin's turn to put his hand on her arm. She found it comforting.

"Gramps made up for it. He taught me how to drive. Came to all my school events. You know, that kind of thing. And then I went away to college. The first year in the dorms was rough. I made friends, but they shifted constantly, and I never really knew where I fit in. Sophomore year, though, I met James."

She sensed Austin's tension, the way his muscles coiled. As if he had any reason to be jealous.

Jealous? Yeah, right. How stupid—to assume he was jealous.

"James was my English Lit professor. In his thirties, handsome in a boyish, intellectual way."

"This doesn't sound promising." He had his gruff tone on, which amused her.

"I saw what I wanted to see." A bug landed on AJ's shirt, and she flicked it off. "But I didn't know it at the time. I went to his office hours to ask about one of our assignments, and he talked to me like I was his equal. I'd expected him to think my questions were dumb, but he didn't. And he told me to come back each week, that his door was always open. So I did."

"Hmph."

"Within a month, we were meeting off campus on the other side of town to discuss assignments. I told myself it was innocent, but I found it exciting. Half the girls in the class had a crush on Professor Donovan, and there I was, alone with James, enjoying his complete attention."

"What a jerk."

"I know." Although her nerves jittered, she forced herself to share the rest. "He told me that after Christmas we could be more open about our relationship. I would no longer be his student then. At the time, we'd been meeting at odd hours and in strange locations. But in January, he still insisted on driving forty-five minutes away for mediocre burritos because he claimed the place had ambience. I knew it would look bad—him dating a student, even if I technically wasn't in his class anymore—but I didn't care. I was so infatuated I actually considered dropping out of college to be with him."

Cassie gave him a nervous glance. He seemed riveted to her tale.

"I'm sure you can guess the rest. He told me he loved me. He claimed that as soon as he accepted a position at a different university, we'd make it official. The stars in my eyes could have blinded an entire county. I was so naive. So trusting."

She peeked at him again. The contours of his face sharpened. Shame sloshed around her core, spilling into the empty places she'd been trying to fill for years.

"Two weeks before the spring semester ended, I strolled across campus to his office. I couldn't wait to tell him I'd worked it out to stay there for the summer instead of coming back here and living with my mom. But before I could knock on his door, I heard voices, so I stayed in the hall. The door opened, and a woman walked out. She could have been a model. She spun around, snapping her fingers, and smiled coyly. Then she grabbed his tie and pulled him close to her. They started kissing. That's when I saw the engagement ring on her finger."

"What did you do?"

"Nothing. It was like one of those nightmares where

you're trying to scream and no sound comes out. The woman tousled his hair and started talking about wedding venues. Then she left. I can still hear the click of her heels down the hall. James saw me then. The look on his face would have been comical if my heart hadn't been broken."

"I can't believe that guy had the nerve to prey on you and lie to you and treat you that way." His hands clenched and unclenched.

"Thank you," she said quietly. "All year I'd been focused on James. I'd grown more isolated, so the aftermath was hard. I couldn't admit to my mom what was going on. I'd already signed a sublease on an apartment nearby for the summer. To be honest, I'd neglected everything that didn't involve James. My grades had slipped. I'd blown off my friends. My faith was dangling by a thread. God felt far away, mostly because I'd slammed the door in His face over and over that year."

"I get it. That's how I was after Dad died." He brought his knees up, resting his forearms on them. "So what happened with the guy?"

His understanding bolstered her. The memory of James's reaction still hurt to this day.

"It must have registered that I'd caught him kissing his fiancée. He basically became a different person. He pulled me into the office and shut the door. Told me I'd misunderstood him, that lots of girls grew attached to their professors, that it wasn't his fault. The way he talked to me was so degrading, like he was patting a puppy on its head. I didn't even argue. I didn't yell. I just left."

Austin put his arm around her shoulders and drew her, still holding AJ, into him for a side hug. "Did you tell the college? The dean? The president?"

She shook her head. "No. No way. I didn't tell anyone. I spent three days crying in my dorm room. My roommate was never there, so I had plenty of time to wallow alone. On day four, I was in line at the cafeteria when I ran into two friends from freshman year. Simone and Lysa. They saved a seat for me. I felt like I was a foreigner. There they were laughing and chatting and trying to engage me in conversation, and I felt like I'd been dropped in from another world. One of them—Lysa, I think—asked if we'd heard that Professor Cutie—that was the campus nickname for James—was leaving. He'd gotten a job at a private college out East. He was moving right after his wedding."

"When was the wedding?"

Why this part was so hard on her, she didn't know. "In two weeks." Her throat felt raw admitting it. "He'd been engaged since Christmas, but no one knew about their engagement until she'd shown up on campus."

"He should be fired." Austin stared ahead, a dangerous glint in his eye. "He should never have a job at a college again."

"I want the whole situation to stay in the past where I left it."

"Have you, though? Left it in the past?" The question was quiet, thoughtful. She stared into his eyes and saw her own fears and pain reflected back. Austin had been through trauma, too.

"I don't know." She wanted to think she'd put it behind her. Tried to avoid thinking about it. Was pushing toward her future instead of reliving the past. "Have you?"

He started to nod, but it became more of a side wobble. "I'm not sure. I don't know if I can ever be the same."

"I get that. I'm not the same, either. I don't think we

should be. We're wiser now. Right?" Her arm began falling asleep, so she adjusted it, causing AJ's head to bob. Then she cradled his upper body, and he let out a contented sigh in his sleep.

"I thought I was wiser, but…" His gaze dropped to her lips, then quickly lifted to the sky. "Yes. I'm wiser. I'm not as lost anymore. For the most part, I know what I need to do."

"Like what?"

"What I'm doing. Taking care of the ranch. Raising AJ."

She kept waiting for an *and* that never came. Tilting her head, more questions pounded her. Why was his name never attached to any of the women around here? Why wasn't he married?

"You don't date, do you?" she asked.

"Don't see the point."

"You have no plans to get married."

"Correct."

"Why?"

"Why would I?"

"For one, you have the most darling, loving, cuddly ball of energy sitting on my lap right now who would probably love to have a mommy, too."

"I'm not getting married just to give AJ a mom."

A point in his favor. Not that he didn't have oodles of them already.

"Okay, then a partner. Someone to weather the ups and downs of life together."

"Yeah, well, I can't count on that. No one seems to be able to weather them when it comes to me."

"What do you mean?"

He looked her in the eyes. His honesty and conviction seared her. "My mom died when I was a kid. My dad died before his time. Even Camila, the strongest woman I knew, died. My brother could have a heart attack any minute. So, no, I'm not looking for a *partner* to weather the storms. I was meant to get through them alone."

She hadn't added up that he'd lost most of the important people in his life. While she wanted to take his hand and assure him she wasn't going anywhere, she couldn't. Sure, she was healthy, in the prime of her life, but she wasn't exactly strong.

For the past year, it felt like she'd been treading water in the middle of the ocean, just waiting for a ship to pass by and pluck her out and take her where she was meant to be.

"I'm sorry you lost so many people you love, Austin." She slipped her hand under his and clasped his fingers.

"I am, too." He turned to her with a small sad smile before letting go of her hand.

Cassie sensed the moment fading. Wished she could gather Austin into her arms and assure him he wasn't meant to be alone. Wished he would say something along the lines of *I don't want to lose you, too.*

But he wasn't going to. While telling him about James was a relief in some ways, it also was a reminder. James had had his own agenda, and Austin did, too.

She'd been a distraction for her professor, someone to boost his ego, to hang on to his every word and play by his rules.

Austin would never treat her that way, didn't need her to boost his ego and barely said enough words to make her hang on to them. But he still set the rules. He'd made it clear he didn't want romance, didn't want a partner.

He wanted a nanny.

Nothing more.

* * *

With a half-moon shining in the horizon and the constellations visible against the black velvet sky, Austin sat on an old rickety wooden chair out on the front porch later that night. He tipped back on the rear legs, hoping the chair wouldn't collapse. Man, he was antsy.

It was time to take charge. No more hemming and hawing and dancing around his problems.

Voices from the past mingled in his mind. Dad's was always the loudest. *This will all be yours someday. You're in charge. I'm counting on you.*

Tears welled up, and he slammed the chair back down on all four legs, reaching for the glass of water he'd set next to him on the porch. Gulped a few drinks down.

His father had always believed in him. He'd learned everything that mattered from the man. How to ride, how to rope, how to treat people, how to be a good brother, how to be a good man.

One of those tears slipped out of the corner of his eye. He swiped it away before it could travel. Then he ground his teeth together, his entire body stiff as a fence pole, as he willed more tears away.

He. Did. Not. Cry.

I miss you, Dad. I need you. I don't know how to get out of this mess. The ranch. Cassie. I don't think I'm the man you wanted me to be.

What would Dad tell him if he were here?

For one, he'd probably clap him on the shoulder and tell him to calm down. That good times came and went. Droughts did, too. The ranch would be okay. He'd ride out the problems and do whatever needed to be done.

What *did* need to be done?

Cassie's pretty smile popped into his head. The way

she'd pull her hair over her shoulder. The way she'd absentmindedly sip her tea while on her phone. Her gentle, loving touch with AJ.

Her hand slipping into Austin's. How rose-petal soft her skin felt, how small her fingers were compared to his.

What she'd told him about her professor had filled him with a fury he still didn't know what to do with. That a man would abuse her trust like that... It was infuriating.

Austin should have taken her in his arms and held her. He should have told her she'd been victimized, that she wasn't to blame. But he'd barely said five words about it—typical—because he hadn't known what to say.

He knew what he'd wanted to say. "You're better off without him. You're the best woman I know."

But those words would have upset the balance of his already topsy-turvy life.

Because he would have kissed her again.

And another kiss would have scrambled his good sense. And who knew what would have come out of his mouth after that?

"I'm getting in too deep with her." He nodded to himself, almost rolling his eyes at the absurdity. He was alone on his porch in the dead of night, talking out loud to himself. He gripped his thighs. "Dad, you're right. It's time to take charge."

He knew what he had to do. Had known it all along. He just didn't want to do it.

On Monday, he'd call the feedlots about selling a third of his herd. Tomorrow, he'd call his friends and ask them if they knew of anyone hiring part-time on the weekends. Hannah and Tess seemed to know everything in Sunrise Bend, and if they didn't know of any job openings, Bridget might have heard something at the coffee shop.

As for Operation Make Cassie Stay? He only had a week left, and his heart wasn't in it. She deserved the life she wanted, the one she'd gone to school for, the one in the city where she could use her knowledge and business skills in a job that fulfilled her. There, she'd find a man who would appreciate her.

Austin appreciated her.

But he couldn't offer her what she wanted. What she needed.

He'd told her about his father and Camila. Hadn't left anything out. Except the one thing he feared would hurt those he loved.

Austin balked in an emergency.

How could he look a woman—any woman—in the eyes and expect them to have a future with him if all he could do was stand rooted in place when danger struck?

He couldn't. They were better off without him. And he was better off alone.

Chapter Ten

She could take the hint.

With a loud ripping noise, Cassie unrolled packing tape and applied it to the bottom of another box. She didn't know why she'd been putting off packing up her room, but she wasn't any longer. After her and Austin's conversation yesterday, there truly was no reason for her to stay.

Allison would be a terrific nanny for AJ. The thought hurt Cassie's heart so much she was surprised it was still beating.

But the child wasn't hers. He would never be hers.

Austin wasn't getting married. Ever.

She understood...kind of. He'd lost too many loved ones. Didn't want to lose another. Therefore, he wouldn't let himself get close enough to lose someone else.

Yeah, she understood. Wasn't she the same in many ways?

Flipping the box over, she sat back on her heels and scanned the room. The posters from high school were long gone. She'd replaced them with a photo collage of small Polaroids she'd taken over the past several years.

Rising, she winced at the muscles twitching in her calves and studied each picture before plucking them one by one off the string full of clips keeping them in place.

The one of her and Mom when she'd moved into her dorm freshman year made her smile. Gramps had taken the picture in front of the dorm after a sweaty laughter-and-argument-filled morning.

There were snapshots of her and Simone. Brandi and Lysa. The diner they would gravitate to for cheap pancakes after a late-night study marathon. There were other pictures as well. Mountains and fireworks. Red clay surrounding the highway on their way to an outdoor concert. A random cowboy tipping his hat at a rodeo.

When all the photos were down and she'd examined each one, Cassie slipped the pile into a plastic bag and set it on her dresser.

There hadn't been one picture of her father in the pile. Not surprising, since she hadn't seen him in years—and didn't want to. He clearly felt the same.

No pictures of James, either. They'd never taken any. She'd wanted to get a photo of them together, but it could have gotten him into trouble.

Yes, James had been wrong to toy with her emotions. But she'd been wrong to date him, too.

At nineteen, she'd been careless. Needy. Lost.

After tiptoeing around the pile of half-packed boxes, she perched on the edge of her bed, her shoulders slumping.

God, all this time I blamed myself for falling for the wrong guy. Yes, I blamed him for misleading me, too. But I didn't want to admit—even to myself—that it was wrong for me to date my professor.

Maybe she'd needed time to get to this point. Or

maybe she was ready because she'd finally talked about it. Austin had been the right person to tell. He hadn't judged her. He might have even understood.

That's what's eating at me. All the warning signs were there with James, but I ignored them because I was selfish. I'm sorry. Will You forgive me?

Expecting to feel shame, guilt, even sadness, she was surprised at the bright sensation growing inside her, as if someone had wiped the dirt off a window, exposing sunlight.

It buoyed her, but her conscience was whispering, "You're falling for the wrong guy…again."

Her feelings for Austin—the things that drew her to him—weren't healthy. She'd been trying to avoid unhealthy relationships for years, but she kept falling into the same trap.

Like with her father, like with James, she wanted Austin's approval. His acceptance. She wanted to be important to him.

Austin had been transparent with her yesterday, telling her things he hadn't told anyone besides his brother. It had gone straight to her head. Made her weak-kneed at the thought of being his confidante. Of being special to him.

With a shake of her head, she straightened. Then she pulled back her shoulders and stood.

She had changed. She wasn't careless anymore. Or needy. Or lost. Or selfish.

She no longer ignored her conscience.

Austin wasn't the man for her. Yes, she suspected he had strong feelings for her. Why else would he have kissed her after the wedding? Why else would he have shared his secrets yesterday?

But he wasn't going to act on them. Wouldn't allow himself to—it was obvious. So rather than make a fool of herself the way she had with James, she had to accept reality and leave.

It was the right thing to do for her peace of mind.

Methodically, she packed the contents of her desk, throwing out old supplies she'd never use again.

She couldn't act on her feelings for Austin. It wouldn't be fair to him. He was too vulnerable with the ranch crisis, a toddler to raise and his insistence on staying single. He'd told her who he was, and she'd listened. Even if she didn't like it.

When the box was full, she taped it closed and labeled it with a Sharpie. Then she emptied her closet shelves, sorting everything into piles.

Eventually, she'd get over her attraction to him. She would. It would take time, but she'd move on with her life without him in it.

She'd had plenty of practice moving on—with her dad and then James.

A knock on the front door gave her an excuse to take the break she needed. As Cassie navigated the maze of boxes to get out of her bedroom, she thought about how great it was going to be to have her own apartment. She'd be an adult again instead of stuck in this limbo she was in.

She opened the door, and to her surprise, Bridget and Mac stood on her doorstep. The sunshine created a radiant effect around them.

"Hi, Cassie," Bridget said with a smile. The slim brunette always had an air of calm about her. She made people feel welcome, and Cassie had been around her enough to know the residents of Sunrise Bend enjoyed sharing their lives with her, as she always seemed to understand and sympathize with them.

"What are you two doing here?" Cassie waved for them to come inside. "Come in. Sit down."

They all headed to the living room. As the couple settled in on the couch, Cassie took a seat on an accent chair.

"Sorry to stop by unannounced, but Hannah and Tess mentioned you might be looking for an apartment." Bridget glanced at Mac, who couldn't seem to tear his eyes away from his new bride. "Mac and I discussed it, and we were wondering if you'd be interested in mine? The apartment above Brewed Awakening is big. Two bedrooms. One bath. Laundry room, too."

"Oh." Cassie had not expected this. She couldn't say she was shocked, since the topic had come up before, but they seemed eager for her to rent it. She wrinkled her nose. "I'm sorry. I'm not looking for a place here. I'm moving to Colorado Springs."

"Did you get a job already?" Bridget's face fell. "I mean, it would be great for you if you did."

"Not yet." These two were so nice. "I'm still interviewing."

She brightened. "See? You should come tour it."

"Uh…"

"Take a break." Mac's smile lit his eyes. "We'll buy you a coffee, too. I've got an in with the owner."

Bridget shook her head in mock disgust. "He thinks he's funny."

Cassie snorted out a chuckle.

"Hey, she laughed." Mac arched his eyebrows.

Bridget pretended to smack his arm, then turned to Cassie. "Seriously, though, why don't you have a look?"

"Uh, why?" She didn't see the point, although she

was curious to get a glimpse of what it looked like. The price was likely a fraction of rent on the apartments she was checking out in Colorado.

"Why? We're still on board with Operation Make Cassie Stay." Mac grinned.

She frowned, trying to wrap her mind around what he was saying.

"Mac!" Bridget gave him a wide-eyed glare. "You weren't supposed to say anything."

"What? Why?"

"Because it sounds weird." She addressed Cassie again. "It's not weird, I promise. We just all like you and want you to stay in Sunrise Bend."

Emotions she hadn't experienced in a long time resurfaced. Warm, fuzzy feelings. Gratitude, mainly.

They liked her. They wanted her to stay.

"And Austin does *not* want to hire another nanny." Mac opened his hands.

Another emotion crashed into her, drowning out the good. Disappointment.

They wanted her to stay…for Austin. Not because they liked her.

"I don't care if he hires another nanny or not, *I* want you here." Kindness gushed from Bridget. "I feel like we're finally getting to know you—and believe me, I get that you needed to take care of your grandfather— but now you're leaving so soon. It's bumming me out."

And the good feelings roared back.

What if she did stay? Not for Austin or AJ. But for herself?

She'd be near her mom. She'd have people her age whom she genuinely liked to do things with.

The dream life always included her own apartment.

And a coffee shop nearby. And friends. Sunrise Bend offered all of the above.

"Why not?" She shrugged. "Can't hurt to look, right?"

Bridget squeezed Mac's hand. "Great! Let's go."

Austin carried AJ on his hip as he strolled down the sidewalk to Brewed Awakening Saturday afternoon. He'd been on the phone for the past hour with Randy, then Sawyer, Blaine and Jet. The only person he still needed to talk to was Mac, who wasn't answering his phone. Jet had told him to check at the coffee shop. It was no secret Mac didn't want to be far from his new bride. Which suited Austin fine since she, technically, was the one who would know if anyone around town needed part-time help.

Besides, every now and then, he craved one of Brewed Awakening's salted caramel lattes. He opened the door and waved to Joe Schlock, who ran the store on Saturdays, as he strode to the counter.

"Howdy, Austin. How's life treating you these days? And how's the young 'un here?"

"I've got no complaints." He had a lot of them, actually, but what was the use in airing them? His troubles weren't special. All the ranchers were dealing with the drought. As for his personal problems, they'd work themselves out. He hoped they would, at least. "AJ's good, aren't you, buddy?"

"Yum!" He pointed to the large frosted sugar cookies with sprinkles.

"See what I mean?" Austin grinned. "Give the kid a cookie, and all his problems disappear."

"I wish it worked that way for grown-ups." Joe chuckled. "Mandy Ball was in earlier, and she has had a time of it with that clunker of hers. I told her to take it to John to get it looked at, but she just shook her head. Too expensive. I think she needs to start looking for a replacement. No sense pouring all that money into something bound to break down again, you know?"

"Sorry to hear that." He didn't know Mandy well and didn't really care about her clunker. Shame pinched him. He should care, right? But he didn't have the bandwidth at the moment. "I'll take a salted caramel latte and one of those banana muffins. Chocolate milk for this guy. Oh, and a sugar cookie."

"Coming right up." After Joe rang him up and turned away to make his latte, Austin scanned the place. No sign of Bridget or Mac. Just a couple of middle-aged women in the corner and a group of high school kids huddled around a table, laptops open. They must be studying. From the giggles and joking around, though, he doubted much learning was getting done.

The front door opened and the overhead bell clanged. He glanced back to see who entered.

Mac, Bridget…and Cassie? They were all laughing about something.

"Hey, just who I wanted to see." Grinning, Mac strode his way.

The trio approached as Bridget told Cassie about the September specials. Then Bridget skirted around the counter to ask Joe if he needed any help, which he didn't.

Five minutes later, Austin found himself sandwiched between Cassie and AJ in his high chair, with Mac and Bridget all googly-eyed with each other across from them.

"Like I was saying, you'd be doing us a favor if you decided to rent it." Bridget took another sip from her mug as she gave her full attention to Cassie. Austin was listening with half an ear to Mac as he jabbered on about the new cancer satellite center set to open next year.

"I didn't expect the rent to be so low." Cassie toyed with her to-go cup. "And you weren't kidding when you said it was spacious."

Wait… The apartment… Was Cassie considering staying? A burst of hope filled his heart. He hadn't realized she might actually be willing to stay.

His latte tasted better, sweeter than it had a moment ago.

"You haven't heard a word I said." Mac narrowed his eyes, snapping his fingers near Austin's face. "What's going on with you?"

"Nothing." He brushed crumbs from AJ's shirt, hoping no one could see the heat rising up his neck. "Tell me again about the center."

Mac launched back into the details, and Austin proceeded to ignore him again. He listened to Bridget and Cassie, but they had moved on to discuss Tess's upcoming due date and how adorable Madeline, Sienna's baby, was.

He'd missed the good stuff. The important stuff.

And there was no way he was asking Mac or Bridget about part-time jobs with Cassie sitting here.

"Oh, Mac, we have to go." Bridget stood abruptly, giving an apologetic smile to Cassie. "We're meeting Kaylee. I didn't realize it had gotten so late."

She and Mac stood, said their goodbyes and left him and AJ alone with Cassie.

"What's this about Bridget's apartment?" he asked as nonchalantly as possible.

"What's this about Operation Make Cassie Stay?"

Her pleasant demeanor vanished. The look she flashed him was sharp.

How had she found out about that?

"I don't know what you mean." He lifted his chin.

"I think you do."

His brain tried on all the ways she could have found out. "Did Mac say something?"

Her nod was less hostile. Man, he hated seeing the hurt in her eyes.

"Can you blame them?" he asked softly.

"Who?"

"My friends—your friends, too."

She glanced at AJ as he continued to dip his index finger into a glob of frosting and lick it, but she didn't respond.

"We all like you, Cassie. You're amazing with my son. You're fun to be around. None of us want you to leave."

She swallowed, refusing to meet his eyes. Then she looked at him. "I think you're being manipulative."

Manipulative? He stiffened. "That's not fair."

"I think it is." Her brown eyes glistened. "You want me to be AJ's nanny. You don't want to adjust to someone new."

"Well, put like that…yeah." He stretched his neck side to side. He hadn't made a secret about it, so why was she mad?

"Then you have your friends treat it like it's some sort of game."

"Like I said, they're your friends, too." He wasn't letting her get away with blaming it all on him. "So what if they're trying to help me get you to stay?"

"You don't get it."

"You're right. I don't. Why are you mad?"

"Put it this way," she said, splaying her fingers as she placed them flat on the table. "I'm just going about my life, thinking these people are taking an interest in me. That means they must like me. I assume all their attention, not to mention the discount on rent, isn't due to an ulterior motive. If I hadn't known about their so-called operation before, how do you think I'd feel when I *did* find out? I'd be mortified."

"It's not like that." What was he supposed to say? She was taking this the worst possible way and blowing it way out of proportion. "They're not trying to pull a fast one on you. Besides, now you know. No need to feel anything but good that they want you to stay."

"I don't feel good."

He sighed, staring up at the corner of the ceiling. "I don't know how to fix this."

"You can't." She got up to leave.

"Cassie, wait."

Her fingers tapped the back of the chair, and the stare she gave could have probably burned a hole straight through the middle of his forehead if he didn't have such a thick skull.

"It wasn't my idea," he said. "When they came up with it, they all seemed happy, and I figured it couldn't hurt. Will you take it for what it is? An innocent pact? We all want you here."

"Do you, now?" The skeptical glare made her look even prettier.

"Yeah, we do."

"What about you, Austin? Do *you* want me to stay?"

"You know I do. I've never said or given you any reason to think otherwise. Yes, Cassie, I want you to stay."

Disappointment settled on her features like a layer of

dust. She gave him a tight smile, then kissed the top of AJ's head. "I've got to go. I'll see you later."

This time he didn't try to prevent her from leaving. The conversation had gone way over his head, anyway. He'd only dig himself in deeper if she stayed.

But something told him he'd already dug himself a hole too deep to climb out of—and it had nothing to do with Operation Make Cassie Stay.

It was an impossible situation. The same as everything else in his life.

Had she overreacted? Cassie followed along with the reading as she sat next to her mother at church the following morning. Carlos sat on the other side of Mom. When Mac had let it slip about their operation to make her stay, she'd been shocked—in a bad way. Bridget, of course, had made her feel better. And when Mac and Bridget had given her the tour of the apartment, she'd found herself warming to them even more.

They clearly meant her no harm.

Then Mac had tossed out a ridiculously low number for rent, and the doubts crept back in. By the time they'd gone down to Brewed Awakening for coffees, Cassie had spotted Austin, and all the hurt and anger she'd been bottling up had risen to the surface.

Nothing Austin said had been wrong. There was no reason for her to be mad that his friends liked her and wanted her around.

So why did she feel so twitchy and upset?

Because they don't want you to stay for the reasons you want them to. Admit it. You're falling for him. You wouldn't mind being his plus-one for their Friday night get-togethers. And they all—including Austin—see you as the nanny, not as a potential girlfriend for him.

The congregation rose to pray, and she prayed, too, but her heart wasn't in it.

God, I'm so confused. Why am I mad? Because people I like want me to stick around? That doesn't even make sense.

Three weeks ago, she'd thought moving out of state would solve all her problems. She'd get a good job. Reconnect with friends. Forget about Austin. Relegate AJ to a less prominent place in her heart.

But since then, the waters had grown muddy. She couldn't stand the thought of leaving AJ. She liked Austin's friends more and more. And the idea of finding a job in a big city didn't excite her as much as she thought it would.

It's my decision to leave. No one is forcing me. I could stay here if I really wanted to.

She could move into Bridget's old apartment. Hang out on Fridays with everyone. Go to church with Mom and Carlos like she was right now.

Yeah, and what about the real reason you're leaving? Hello, the job? Your future?

She could find a job in her field here. It might not pay as well or be as prestigious as one in the city, but would it matter? It would allow her to create some emotional distance between herself and AJ and Austin.

Except she didn't want distance from them.

"Those who put their hope in the Lord will never be put to shame." The pastor's words jolted her. "Even when the hope feels misplaced. Even when life doesn't make sense."

Her life didn't make sense, that was for sure.

It would, though.

As soon as she left town.

She'd put all these doubts and desires behind her.

It would all work out. It had to.

She'd prayed. She'd asked God to lead her to the right apartment. She'd asked Him to provide a job.

"God wants you to rely on Him. He loves you."

God, You do love me, don't You?

God had protected her throughout her life, even when she'd done stupid things. He'd been there when she'd dealt with the consequences of her mistakes, and He'd gently led her back to Him, back to the Bible, back to church.

If only her life could be easier.

Okay, what am I supposed to do? I thought I knew, but now...

A hymn began, and she sang along. When it ended, her thoughts went back to staying in Sunrise Bend.

It would be a mistake. She knew in her heart it would be the wrong choice, just as she'd known dating James was wrong. The rosy future she was painting here would have a dark cloud over it.

She was too drawn to Austin. She needed a clean break. A fresh start. A good job. Benefits. A life of her own.

Even if it broke her heart in the process.

Chapter Eleven

Why had he convinced himself Cassie's idea for the ranch wouldn't work?

Monday evening Austin didn't even pretend to watch the football game blaring from the television. Sitting on the couch, he stared at the laptop balancing on his thighs and, over and over, flipped the flash drive into the air.

He'd almost called the feedlot three times today. Each time, something held him back.

Selling a third of the cattle would be final. Once he made the call, he could no longer fantasize that the ranch would be okay.

So he hadn't called. Even though all weekend he'd told himself it was mandatory. Nonnegotiable.

Tomorrow. He'd force himself to do it in the morning.

Another call he'd failed to make? The one to Allison to formally offer her the job. Cassie's final day would be this Friday, and he'd officially be without a babysitter. But whenever he'd picked up his phone to contact Allison, his finger would hover over the screen, and he'd freeze, only to slip his phone back into his pocket.

This indecision could make or break him.

It felt similar to his reaction to his dad's death, to the lethargy when Camila got him out of the bar, to the out-of-body feeling he got when he'd first held AJ after officially becoming the baby's sole parent.

Each of those moments had changed his life forever. And these phone calls would, too. Because once he made them, he'd have to accept the fact that Cassie would no longer be in his life.

When she'd arrived this morning, things had been silent, icy between them. He'd hurt her feelings at the coffee shop, and he didn't know how to make it right with her. He didn't know how to make anything right.

What did he have to offer a smart, gorgeous woman like her?

A failing ranch and a job babysitting his son. A job that didn't meet her needs.

He wished he could give her more—the partnership she'd mentioned, the one where a couple weathered life's storms together.

For a year, he'd admired her, and for the past month, the admiration had shifted to more. He was falling for her, and he didn't know if there was a way out. The only remedy he could think of was to keep his distance. And how could he do that if she stayed here?

That was why he had to sell part of the herd, hire Allison and find a part-time job to pay the bills.

Speaking of jobs…he'd gotten a text this afternoon from Sawyer. He swiped through his messages, found it and reread it. Tess said Big Buck Supermarket is looking for someone to unload trucks on Friday and Saturday nights.

Unloading trucks. Austin could do that. He tossed

plenty of bales of hay around every day. It couldn't be much different.

A knock on the door startled him. The laptop almost flopped onto the floor. He steadied it, then set it to the side and loped over to the door. As soon as he opened it, Randy and Ned surged inside.

"What are you doing here?" Austin let Ned sniff his hand while Randy shut the door.

"Watching the game with you. Hannah's having Rachel and Sunni over for—" he lifted his fingers in air quotes "—cupcake time. Don't get me wrong, my nieces are cute, but I missed half of last week's game because they were making necklaces out of beads and insisted I make one, too."

"Why aren't you wearing it?"

"Very funny." The look of disgust Randy gave him would have put a lesser man in his place. Austin just grinned, padded back to the living room and reclaimed his spot on the couch. Randy settled into the recliner, kicking up the footrest. Ned sat on the floor beside him. "Ahh. This is more like it."

"Want something to eat? Drink?"

"Do you have any popcorn?"

"I do. Extra butter?"

"Duh. Of course."

Austin went to the kitchen and tossed a bag of popcorn into the microwave, pressed the button and returned to the living room just as the rival team ran in a touchdown.

"Oh, no!" Austin yelled. "What are they doing? How could they let him run through like that?"

"Where was the defense?" Randy threw his hands on top of his head.

They complained about the play calling until the microwave beeped. Austin hurried to the kitchen, poured the bag into two bowls and handed Randy one on his way back to the couch.

"Oh, I forgot to tell you." Randy pointed a piece of popcorn his way. "Hannah said the elementary school needs bus drivers and help in the cafeteria."

"No." The thought of being around all those kids positively shriveled his bones.

A grin spread across his face. "Why not?"

"Come on. I don't have the patience to drive a bus full of rowdy kids."

"Okay, what about serving up mac and cheese and sloppy joes?" The taunting in his tone rubbed Austin the wrong way.

"Ha ha." He glared at his brother.

"A hairnet would look good on you."

He threw a handful of popcorn at Randy. Most of it landed on the floor, and after his brother stopped laughing, he signaled his permission for Ned to eat the kernels.

"Seriously, though, Austin. I've been thinking about the ranch and getting through the winter and Cassie's idea about selling the beef yourself instead of going the feedlot route."

"Oh, yeah." Why was his heart beating faster?

"Uh-huh." Randy angled his head, thrusting his chin out. "What about my store?"

"What about your store?"

"We could install a couple of freezers there. I get customers from all over. Even other states. I'll tell them it's prime meat from the family ranch. And you could call Gabe at Big Buck Supermarket to see if they'd sell your beef."

Austin tried on the idea and liked it. Randy did have a wide customer base.

"I figure I could fit two large deep freezers in the store where I have the sleeping bags. There's no need for me to keep all the camping gear on display. It takes up too much room there, anyway."

Yes, the wall where the sleeping bags were shelved. Austin could see it.

"I'd pay you a commission, of course," Austin said. "That is, if I decide to try it."

"Nah, this is for the ranch. It's important to me, too. And I don't know why you wouldn't try it. What have you got to lose? Unless you secretly *do* want to wear a hairnet and serve lunch to third graders."

"Nooo." A shudder crawled over his shoulders and down his spine. "No hairnets. No school kids."

The announcers got excited over an interception, and they turned their attention back to the game. Shouted at the television as refs made questionable calls and discussed what teams were most likely to make it to the playoffs.

This was more like it. Football and popcorn and his brother. It was a nice break from the stress of everything else.

"I guess our operation didn't work, huh?" Randy asked.

"What?"

"To make Cassie stay."

"Oh. That. Yeah." He leaned forward, letting his elbows rest on his splayed knees.

"Are you okay with it?"

"No, I'm not. Obviously, I want her here for AJ's sake.

I mean, I'll be calling Allison Jones tomorrow and offering her the job, but it won't be the same."

"Do you only want Cassie here for AJ's sake?" The question sounded innocent, but underlying currents lingered.

"Yeah, why?"

He shrugged. "You two get along well. She's a good friend to you and, I don't know, I guess I saw what the guys mentioned. You know, when we had the cookout a few weeks ago? You two just seemed to fit together."

As much as he wanted to deny it, he didn't. This was Randy. His brother. His best friend.

"She is a good friend, and I'm not going to lie, I'm attracted to her. More than that, really. I like her more than I've ever liked any woman."

"Have you told her?"

"Me? Nah." He shook his head, staring at the carpet before meeting Randy's eyes. "I'm way too old for her."

His eyebrows rose. "Six, seven years? You're hardly robbing the cradle."

"I've got too much going on. The ranch. Money problems. A kid."

Randy's mouth formed an O. "I forgot. She doesn't know about AJ."

"About that…" He winced, rubbing the back of his neck. "She knows about Camila. I told her."

He stared at him in surprise. "She knows?"

"Yeah."

"How did I not see this?" Understanding dawned on his face. He jabbed his index finger at Austin. "You're in love with her."

He opened his mouth to deny it, but he couldn't.

"Doesn't matter," Austin said. "I don't have what she

wants. She's young. She already sacrificed a year of her life to help her mom out with her grandfather. Cassie wants a business job. Her own apartment. A bigger life than I can offer her—a bigger life than Sunrise Bend can, too."

"Are you sure about that?" Randy had snapped the footrest down and was leaning forward.

"Yes."

"Because she seemed pretty happy hanging out with all of us. At the wedding. At our house. And her mom's here, too. I don't know, maybe she does need more, but it's not what either of you think."

"Then what is it, Randy?" He didn't mean to be snippy, but his brother didn't know the first thing about the situation. "She was real clear about wanting to put her business degree to use."

"Which she did. Her idea for the ranch was impressive. Did you tell her it was?"

"No."

"Austin, sometimes I think your skull is made of granite. She needs to know you respect her ideas."

"I do. I respect her."

Randy sighed. "You haven't had a girlfriend since high school, so what's holding you back? Cassie's perfect for you, and if you can't see it, I don't know how to open your eyes."

Cassie *was* perfect for him. But he wasn't perfect for her.

"Let's just drop it." Austin gestured to the television. "The game's back on."

Randy was right about one thing. There was something holding him back. His own indecision, his fear of failing when faced with a crisis.

What woman would want a man like that?

Even if Cassie could look past it, he couldn't. She deserved a man who would take charge, protect her. And he was not that man.

Cassie stared at her phone Tuesday afternoon as she paced Austin's living room. She'd gotten the call she'd been waiting for—the one offering her a job. Austin would arrive any minute, and she dreaded the conversation they were about to have.

A tech company in Colorado Springs wanted to hire her for an entry-level position. The pay wasn't great, but the job would get her foot in the door and give her the experience she needed. She could start in two weeks. All she had to do was call Simone to take her up on her offer of letting her stay there until an apartment became available.

That...and...tell Austin she'd gotten the job.

She padded into the kitchen and headed straight to her tote bag. She took out the folder she'd brought. It contained the printouts of the scratch-and-dent freezers, the information about the butchers and the logos she'd created. Although she hadn't planned on giving him any of it—he certainly wasn't interested in her opinion—she wanted him to have it. Just in case he changed his mind.

Last night her feelings had shifted while she'd finished packing the contents of her room. She didn't want there to be a strain between them. No hard feelings before she left.

She cared about him too much to let her stubborn pride get in the way of what could be the answer to *his* prayers.

So she was giving him the folder. What he did with it was none of her business.

But if only he'd listen to her. If only he would try it her way...

Shaking her head, she debated heating up a mug of water for tea. No, her nerves were too frayed. Every little noise made her jump and look to the mudroom door.

She was under no illusions. This conversation would not go well.

As if punctuating her thoughts, the door opened and her heart thumped as she listened to Austin go through his routine. Then he entered the kitchen, and her tummy tipped over.

Rumpled hair, scruff on his tanned face, a gleam in his gray eyes. His muscular frame moved with ease—he was familiar. She knew what his moves would look like before he made them.

She wanted to go up and wrap her arms around him and ask him about his day. Wanted to be like an old married couple, not that she knew much about them. The thought sounded nice, though.

But she stayed rooted where she was, trying to figure out how to say what needed to be said.

"You're not drinking tea." Frowning, he pointed to where she normally sat. "Is something wrong?"

Yes, something's wrong. I'm falling so hard for you I might break.

"I'm fine." She faked a bright smile. "Are you in a hurry? Busy right now?"

"No, why?" He turned to take a glass out of the cupboard. Then he filled it with water and faced her again.

"I have news."

"What is it?"

"I was offered a job today."

His body went completely still. It reminded her of when she played freeze tag as a kid.

"It's in Colorado Springs, like I've been hoping for." Why was her voice so shaky? "Entry level. A good opportunity, though."

He didn't so much as blink.

"My friend Simone offered to let me stay with her until I find an apartment."

Why wasn't he saying anything?

Flustered, she remembered the folder in her hand. "Oh, here. I printed these out for you."

She held it out to him, but he continued staring at her and made no move to take the folder. She set it on the counter next to him. Disappointment weighed on her shoulders.

"I found scratch-and-dent freezers. Majorly discounted ones. If you look through the sheets, you'll see the prices and where to order them. They're from different companies."

He hadn't so much as twitched. It unnerved her.

"I also made a list of butchers. Some from other towns." She rubbed her clammy hands down the sides of her jeans. "Toyed with some logos. You don't have to use them. I mean, who am I kidding? I know you aren't planning on using them. This—" she waved her hands to the folder "—doesn't make sense. It's not a sure thing. It's scary and out there. But…it's an option, and I want you to know I do appreciate you sharing the business side of the ranch with me. I'm sure it wasn't easy for you."

She stopped talking and frowned, waiting—hoping—he'd say something. Anything.

But he didn't.

"I should go." She grabbed the tote bag and purse. Other words—important ones—rushed to her tongue, but she couldn't let them out. Refused to admit to more.

If he had given her any indication he appreciated the research she'd given him, maybe she could have gathered the courage to be honest with him about her feelings. To at least hint at them.

But his silence defeated her, angered her. Why was she dragging this out? "I'll start explaining to AJ tomorrow that he'll have a new nanny soon. You should, too. I'll… I'll just be going."

She flicked him one more glance, then stiffly made her way to the door, not bothering to look back to see if he'd followed her. She knew he hadn't. She would have heard his steps.

When she got into her car and shut the door, she tried to catch her shaky breath as she started the engine.

If she had any doubts about how Austin felt about her, his response erased them.

He didn't care about her. Not the way she cared about him.

It was good that she'd gotten the job offer. Working here was turning her into the old Cassie. The one who deluded herself into thinking a man actually respected her and wanted a real relationship with her.

At least Austin had never lied to her. He'd told her straight up that he wasn't interested in romance or marriage.

But what about love?

She drove down the long, winding driveway and could no longer hold back the tears. Her last day might be Friday, but today had been the real goodbye.

The pressure of the past month caught up with her.

Time to banish her foolish dreams of having more with Austin. She doubted she'd ever get love right. She simply wasn't cut out for it.

As soon as he heard Cassie's car driving away, his body sagged.

It had happened again.

Confronted with a crisis, he'd frozen. Had been unable to respond. His mind had registered everything she was saying, but it was as if a swarm of bees buzzed around her words, making it impossible for him to process them or react.

The hurt in her eyes had crushed him. The pain in her tone—the uncertainty—made him feel shorter than an inch tall.

Why couldn't he have taken two steps forward, pulled her into his arms and given her a hug? Told her he appreciated all the work she'd done to help his ranch? Assured her that her ideas were good, even if they did scare him?

Why couldn't he at least have made a last-ditch effort to get her to stay?

He'd blown it. Again.

Dropping his face into his hands, he ran his fingers through the hair near his temples.

It wouldn't have made a difference. She still would have left. He knew it the same as he knew when a cow was about to give birth or when snow was ready to fall.

He couldn't give her what she wanted, and he didn't blame her for leaving.

What if you'd told her the truth, though? That you need her. Not just for AJ. For you.

He guessed he'd never know.

After rounding the counter, he sat on one of the stools.

He felt like he was ninety years old. His heart had shriveled up like a raisin. His joints ached. His lungs felt heavy, too heavy to breathe.

Everything he'd been putting off no longer mattered.

Calling the feedlot. Calling Allison. Calling the supermarket for the job. Each call had always been inevitable.

Him failing to keep Cassie here had been, too.

He took out his phone and found the feedlot number. Called it. It rang and rang. Went to voice mail.

"Hi, Larry, it's Austin Watkins. I'm interested in selling some of my cattle. Give me a call back when you have time." He left his number and hung up.

Then he found Allison's contact and called her. Same thing. It rang several times before going to voice mail. "Hi, Allison, it's Austin Watkins. I'm calling about the nanny position. Give me a call back when you have time."

Making these calls was going as well as the rest of his life—as usual, he was a day late and a dollar short.

He called the supermarket and asked for Gabe, only to be told he wasn't in and could they take a message? He left his number and hung up.

The folder stared at him. It was shiny and purple with a small pink heart in the bottom corner. And for some reason the heart seemed to shine.

Austin slid the folder his way and opened it. Drew his eyebrows together as he took out the stack of printouts. Page after page of discounted freezers greeted him. There had to be thirty. And the prices? Rock-bottom.

He shuffled through them again, making sure he wasn't reading them wrong or missing anything.

Nope. Cheap freezers. Dozens of them.

The other side of the folder contained a sheet of paper with six butchers and their contact information. He recognized two names. One of them had been a friend in high school who'd moved to a nearby town long ago.

Beneath the paper with the butchers were pages of graphics with names and logos.

A lump formed in his throat.

She'd done all this. In her free time. Even after he'd dismissed her research.

Cassie was so much wiser than him. So much more confident about taking chances.

The incredible woman saw the possibilities. Sure, she overestimated his ability to learn how to type things into a spreadsheet. But the fact that she considered him capable of doing any of this was humbling.

How could he let her leave?

He had to tell Cassie he was falling in love with her.

She was probably halfway home by now. Should he wait until AJ woke up?

No, he'd just chicken out.

He was going now. A phone call wouldn't cut it. This conversation was happening in person. He'd figure out what to say while he drove. And he'd pray he hadn't already ruined everything.

Chapter Twelve

Five miles had done nothing to take away the pain. Cassie couldn't stop the tears from falling. Even the sky had grown overcast. Why did she keep putting her hopes in men who were emotionally unavailable? Why wasn't she ever enough for them?

Austin probably thought she was too young for him. That she didn't understand how the real world worked. He'd never had any intention of using her ideas. Probably hadn't even opened the spreadsheets she created, let alone entered any data into them.

Why did she always get men and relationships so wrong?

Relationships. Ha. Austin had never pretended he wanted more than a nanny. She'd simply fooled herself into thinking there *could* be more.

She kept one hand on the steering wheel and wiped her cheek with the other.

What about the kiss? You didn't imagine that. You weren't the one who initiated it. That was all him.

She hadn't exactly recoiled or pulled away from it, though. No, the kiss had been mutual.

Too bad her feelings for him weren't.

Keeping her eyes on the road, Cassie fumbled in her purse for a tissue. Found one. Blew her nose. And a fresh batch of sobs began.

If it weren't for AJ, she'd never go back to the ranch.

Three more days. She had no idea how she'd get through them.

Austin's stony silence replayed in her mind. Maybe she should have told him she'd grown close to him. Close enough to be his girlfriend. Closer even than that.

She was falling in love with him. She could see a wonderful future with him for the rest of their days. Not as a nanny, but as his wife.

She choked down another cry. He didn't want a wife. He'd lost so many loved ones. He'd barricaded his heart off to love.

Why hadn't she taken his warning at face value? If only she hadn't agreed to review the ranch's books, she wouldn't have spent so much time with him. Wouldn't have gotten so wrapped up in his business. Wouldn't have wanted to help him with the ranch so badly.

Wouldn't have fallen so hard for him.

Thud.

What…? Something hit the car. She barely had time to register it as the car spun out, tires squealing. Then another thud, this time at the back—or was it the front? All she heard was a crunch of metal.

Screeeech. She tried to steer, but she'd lost control.

The car spun and spun, and she watched in horror as the world spiraled. Her neck jostled, and sagebrush scratched the doors until the vehicle came to an abrupt stop. Her forehead slammed against the steering wheel. And everything went black.

* * *

He would apologize. Tell her everything he'd been too scared to say. Austin strapped AJ into the car seat in the back of the truck. The boy clutched his blankie with one hand and rubbed his tired eyes with the other. Austin had brought a sippy cup and animal crackers in the diaper bag, but he hoped the boy would fall right back to sleep.

His pulse raced and thoughts tumbled as he forced himself not to speed down the driveway. Clouds were moving in fast. Looked like it might actually rain for once. Little good it would do now.

He took a left onto the road leading into town. What was he going to say to her when he got to her house? What if her mom was there?

This was going to be awkward. He wasn't the best speaker on a good day. His nerves were shot as it was.

Just tell her you want her to stay. Tell her you're not sure if you're ready for a relationship, but you're willing to try.

Yeah, that speech would make any woman want to stick around. How dumb could he get?

He drummed his thumbs against the steering wheel and tried to come up with a better plan. Checked the rearview. AJ had conked out again, thankfully.

What if he told her he loved her?

His gut clenched. Wasn't ready to go there yet.

What if... What was that? He squinted. The lonely stretch of road was surrounded by prairie with sagebrush dotting the sides. Something in the distance looked out of place, though. Instinctively, he tightened his grip on the wheel.

That's when he noticed the car.

Cassie's car.

Sideways.

Smashed.

He floored it. His heartbeat pounded. *Boom. Boom. Boom.* Silent prayers of *please* repeated over and over in his head. As he neared, the situation became obvious. A few deer must have crossed the road while she was driving. A doe, unmoving, lay off to the side. Another deer was in the middle of the road. She must have hit them both.

A burning sensation charred his throat as he parked off to the side, slammed the door shut and raced to Cassie's car. Dents and scratches were everywhere. He tried to open the front door, but it was jammed. He could see her in there, her head on the steering wheel. She was clearly unconscious.

No! Please, God, let her be okay!

He yanked and yanked on the door, and finally, it gave way.

"Cassie? Can you hear me?" He tenderly swept her hair back and tried to assess her injuries. After gently lifting her head, he bit his tongue when he saw the bump on her forehead, the bruising around her eyes and the blood trickling from her hairline to her ear.

Quickly, he stood and, with shaking fingers, called 911. They answered immediately, and he told them the exact location of the accident, that an ambulance was needed and there were two deer down as well.

Next, he called Randy, asking him to pick up AJ for him so he could follow Cassie to the hospital. Randy confirmed he was leaving now. Finally, he called Cassie's mom and explained the situation. She was understandably upset, which made him feel even worse, but he was glad when she told him she was driving straight to the hospital instead of coming to the scene of the accident. He didn't want her to have to see Cassie like this— bruised, bleeding and unconscious.

Austin jogged back to the truck to check on AJ. Still sleeping. He cracked open the door so he'd hear him if he woke up crying.

Then Austin ran back to Cassie. How could he help her? He checked her pulse—still strong—and gingerly ran his hands over her neck, shoulders, arms and legs for any signs of broken bones. He didn't find any. What if she had internal injuries? Logically, he knew he wasn't supposed to move her, but he couldn't take seeing her slumped over the steering wheel.

He made a split-second decision to get her out of the car. Unbuckled her seat belt, and carefully slipped one arm around her shoulders and the other under her legs. He lifted her slowly, gently in his arms. He eased his bottom to the ground with his back to the car and held her the way he would a child as he willed his tears not to fall.

This was what he got for his inaction earlier. If he hadn't frozen back there when she told him she'd gotten a job, she wouldn't have left when she did. If he had talked to her—even to congratulate her—she would have missed hitting the deer.

She wouldn't have blood on her face now.

She wouldn't be unconscious.

The disabling fear had paralyzed him. And once again, he'd failed to protect someone he loved.

He tenderly swept the hair back from her forehead. Then he squeezed his eyes shut and shook his head.

Why had he ever thought he'd be good for her? That he could consider having a real long-term relationship with her?

God, I love her. I know I don't deserve her, but I love her. Please, let her wake up. Let her be okay.

"Cassie. Can you hear me? Cassie?" Why was she still unconscious? Were her injuries worse than he thought?

Nausea hit him. He'd finally fallen in love. But the hard facts remained. Even if she healed completely, he couldn't have her, not after failing her so badly.

The sound of sirens made him pull himself together. Randy's truck arrived before the ambulance.

If only he weren't such a worthless mess when trouble hit. A full life like his friends had was merely a fantasy. He'd failed the woman he loved. And he'd never forgive himself for it.

Chapter Thirteen

"Oh, praise the Lord, you're okay!" Cassie's mom ran to her bedside in the hospital with Carlos right behind her. "How are you feeling?"

Her bed had been set to an upright position, and she cautiously returned her mom's hug. "I'm sore. My head hurts. My neck, too. But it could have been worse."

"It's good to see you talking, Cassie." Carlos came up to her and took her by the hand. "We were worried about you. I talked to John at the auto shop, and he's getting your car towed over there tonight."

"Thanks, Carlos." She hadn't thought about her car. She winced. "I hope it wasn't totaled."

"Don't worry about it." He smiled kindly and patted her hand again. "Don't give it a second thought. Just concentrate on healing."

"What did the doctors say?" The worry in her mother's eyes comforted her for some odd reason. One thing she'd never questioned was her mom's love.

"Concussion. Whiplash. Bruising, obviously. They're doing X-rays on my back. I have some shoulder pain, but it's likely strained muscles." She tried to swallow, but her mouth was dry. "Is Austin…?" She didn't finish the thought. She had no idea if he even knew she was there.

"I'll go get him." Carlos pivoted and left the room.

"I don't know what happened." Her eyes felt swollen, so she closed them. "Is there water or something to drink?"

Mom reached over and grabbed a foam cup filled with ice water. She held the straw to Cassie's mouth. She took a long drink. That was better.

"You hit two deer on the way home from Austin's. It was a good thing he was driving to town, or you might have been out there for hours." Her mother got choked up. She fanned herself a moment before continuing. "When he called me, I was so scared. But he'd taken care of everything. Called the ambulance. Made sure you didn't have any broken bones. Knowing he was there with you kept me from falling apart."

Wait… Austin had found her? Why had he been driving to town?

Why couldn't she remember anything from the accident?

Her mother continued to talk, but Cassie couldn't concentrate. Snippets of what had happened before the car spun out came back to her. She'd been crying. Hadn't seen the deer run out. Why had she been crying?

Austin. She'd told him about the job, and he hadn't said a word.

He didn't have feelings for her. Or if he did, they weren't strong enough to allow him to take a chance on love with her. He could have asked her to stay, but he hadn't.

She didn't mean as much to him as he did to her.

Austin appeared in the doorway, and her heart leaped.

Mom glanced back at him with a tender smile and went over to give him a hug. "Thank you again for taking care of her. I'll leave you two alone for a while."

As soon as her mother left the room, Austin set his cowboy hat on a table, slid a chair over and sat by her side. He took her hand in his. His dark gray eyes stormed with turbulence as he lifted her hand and kissed the back of it.

"How are you?" he asked quietly. He looked haggard.

"I'll be alright."

"Seriously, Cassie, what's the damage? Are you in a lot of pain?" His concern warmed her.

"I don't feel any pain right now, but when the pain-killers wear off, I'm sure it will be a different story." She told him what the doctors said, and he blew out a long, slow exhalation in obvious relief.

"When I saw your car…" His lips thinned as he shook his head. "Awful." He glanced up at the ceiling. "I'm sorry, Cassie. I shouldn't have let you leave when you did."

"It's not your fault."

"We both know it was. I should have looked through the folder. I should have talked to you about the new job. At the very least, I should have congratulated you, but I didn't."

She withered. She didn't want congratulations. She wanted him to tell her he needed her, loved her. Why couldn't he ask her to turn the job down and stay? To be with him?

"But I just stood there like a wax figure, and I've got to tell you, it wasn't the first time I've done it. I hate that you not only had to see me like that, but that I hurt you, too. I'm embarrassed. I'm an embarrassment." His jaw flexed.

"You're not—"

"I am." He exhaled loudly. "Look, I haven't given you the credit you deserve. Every idea you had about the ranch was good. The spreadsheets and charts? Genius. I don't know how you put them all together, but they revealed more than my own chicken scratch ever could."

Hope flared to life. She didn't have time to think about his odd statement about being an embarrassment. The fact he was praising her efforts meant the world to her.

"I went through the printouts. I never would have thought to check into discounted freezers. I'd already talked to Randy, and he offered to sell the meat in his store. I know you're probably beat up and exhausted, and I don't want to bother you with all this, but I couldn't let you think I didn't listen."

"Austin." She had to get a word in before he started talking again.

"What?"

"Why were you on the road? Why were you the one to find me?"

His gaze fell to the blankets covering her legs, then he looked up, full of despair. "To tell you all the things I just said."

"Only those things?" She had to know. Had to know if he had feelings for her.

"No." He hesitated. "You and I...we've gotten close. I trust you. With AJ. And with knowing the ins and outs of the ranch. And, well, you're the prettiest woman I've ever seen. Your smile is what I see before I fall asleep every night. My feelings for you...they run deep."

Her heart beat faster. Was he actually telling her he loved her? Was he willing to take a chance on being together?

"Colorado is going to be great." His eyes gleamed as he gave her a tight smile. "Congratulations on the job. I know whoever hired you will get their money's worth and more."

What? She blinked. Colorado? Wasn't he just saying he had feelings for her? And now he wanted to ship her off to her new job?

"Austin, I've grown close to you, too."

He shook his head. "I'm no good for you."

"Why do you say that?" All the hope and joy began dissolving like cotton candy in a toddler's hand.

"Because of what you saw earlier." The words came out choppy. "When a crisis hits, I freeze. I don't seem to have the fight-or-flight response. It was like that when I learned my dad died. And the night in the bar when Camila saved me—I was helpless."

"But losing your dad was a shock. And you were drunk during the whole bar thing."

"Yeah, well, explain how I almost dropped AJ when I took custody of him? I was so stunned I tripped and sprained my ankle. I could have crushed him. Look at today. Because of me, you hit two deer. You had blood running down the side of your face." He reached over and lightly touched the bandage on her forehead. "You're bruised and in pain, and it wouldn't have happened if I could have gotten out of my stupor and actually talked to you. I'm sorry, Cassie. I'm sorry."

He stood, and she grabbed his hand, forcing him to linger.

"You weren't responsible for any of it. Not your dad dying. He would have died no matter what. Not what happened at the bar. The guys would have shot up the place whether you were there or not. Not even AJ. I know you. You'd protect him with your life. And today—yeah, I would have liked to have heard your response. I would have liked to have heard you say something—anything— because it hurt telling you all that and you not saying a word."

"I know." He hung his head. "I'm sorry."

"But it wasn't the reason I hit the deer. Maybe I would have hit a different set of deer if we would have talked longer. I don't know. Just stop blaming yourself for my accident. It doesn't even make sense."

"I can't, Cassie." His voice sounded far away. "I can't protect you, and I can't live with myself if my actions— or to be more precise, inactions—hurt you. Today, they hurt you."

"You're afraid of loving someone and losing them. I get it. But please don't push me away."

He closed his eyes, brought his lips to her hand one last time, kissing her knuckles reverently, then released her. "Go to Colorado. Live your dream."

And with that, he walked out.

She didn't know what hurt more. The fact he'd finally admitted he had feelings for her, or the realization he'd never allow himself to act on them.

He'd done the right thing. The noble thing. He could live with himself now.

"This is more than the accident, isn't it?" Randy leaned against the kitchen counter. Austin had driven from the hospital to Randy and Hannah's house to pick up AJ. "You're wound up tighter than the fishing reels in my store."

Austin rested his elbows on the island, where he sat

on one of the stools. Leave it to his brother to see more than he should.

He wanted to confide in Randy, but it would sound stupid. He didn't even know where to start.

"You've gotten close to Cassie, and you were scared when you found her."

"Yeah." He glanced at his brother, surprised he was so nonchalant about it.

"But what I don't know is why you won't just take a chance and tell her how you feel?" Randy stepped forward, pointing to him. "You love her. Don't deny it."

He ground his teeth together. Stupid Randy. Seeing right through him.

"And I think she feels the same about you." Randy resumed his spot leaning against the counter. "Well, Hannah's the one who thinks so, and she knows more than either of us, so it's best to trust her."

Hannah did know a lot. Austin trusted her. But not with this. He was glad she was in the other room watching an animated movie with AJ. Didn't need her weighing in on his life, too. Not now, anyway.

"What I feel doesn't matter." Austin rapped his knuckles on the counter. "I can't take care of her the way she deserves."

"Look, if this is about money…"

"It's not."

"The ranch will survive the drought. It will, Austin. Let's get a few freezers in my store. It will help pay some of the bills."

"I'm ordering them tomorrow."

Randy pumped his fist in the air. "See? You're making decisions, trying new strategies. Feels good, huh?"

Nothing felt good at the moment. He kept seeing

Cassie bruised and bleeding in his arms by the side of the road. He kept feeling pressure in his chest that it was all because of him.

"I left a message with Gabe to call me tomorrow," Austin said. "Unloading trucks a few nights a week will bring in some much-needed cash."

"You don't have to get a job."

"I do, Randy." Was it possible to age fifty years in one day? Because he felt ancient.

"Then work for me."

"You don't have a night shift." He glared at his brother. "I appreciate what you're doing, but no thanks."

Cartoon voices from the television drifted into the kitchen, and as Austin tried to order his thoughts, the scent of cinnamon and apples from a candle near the sink distracted him. The aroma of autumn. Of home. Of warm nights indoors when the weather grew cold.

He took in the room and saw feminine touches everywhere. The framed picture of Hannah and Randy with Ned sitting between them on their wedding day. A dish towel with dogs all over it hanging from the dishwasher handle. Flowers in a vase on the window ledge. This home wrapped people up like a hug in a way his own house didn't.

Having Cassie there every weekday had helped. But now she'd be gone, and Allison being there wouldn't be the same. Not even close.

"So we're not going to talk about it?" Randy asked, pulling out a stool and sitting.

By *it*, Austin assumed he meant Cassie. He lifted one shoulder in a shrug. What did he have to lose? Hadn't he lost all that mattered when he'd walked out of the hospital?

"I told her to go to Colorado. She was offered a job."

Randy looked like he'd been sprayed by a skunk. "Why would you tell her to go? Shouldn't you be begging her to stay?"

"She wants a fuller life. To use her degree. To have her own apartment. Sunrise Bend doesn't have what she wants."

"How do you know what she wants?" Randy opened his hands, moving to face him. "I've seen her with AJ. She loves the kid. I've seen her with you. She likes you. Maybe even loves you."

"But her degree…?" It sounded lame. He didn't know how to explain.

"She gave you some good advice about the ranch, and she wouldn't have gone to all that trouble if it didn't interest her."

"Maybe she needs to work for a big company and live in the city. I'm not going to hold her back." But that wasn't quite true, and he was tired of pretending. If he couldn't be honest with Randy, he had serious problems. His brother had shared his soul with him on more than one occasion.

Austin scraped his bottom lip with his teeth. "You want the truth? I don't trust myself. And today proved I can't."

"What are you talking about?"

"I can't handle a crisis. I freeze up and don't react. My inaction hurts people. It hurt you."

"Where did you come up with that?" Furrows formed in Randy's forehead. "You never hurt me."

"The day Dad died. You called and told me to come back to the house. I could hear the shock in your voice. I booked it back there. I walked in and you were on the phone calling 911. I looked behind you through Dad's open door and saw his body. I froze. Couldn't react."

"You were in shock. What did you expect?"

"There's more." He ignored the comment. "At the bar I told you about. Men with guns came in, Randy. Guns. And I just sat there. Camila had to get me out."

"You'd been drinking all day. You told me that yourself."

His cheek muscle flexed. Randy didn't get it.

"Okay, well, did you ever wonder how I sprained my ankle before I brought home AJ?"

"No." The word came out firm.

"When the social worker handed him to me with the paperwork confirming he was legally mine, I froze. Had no awareness of my surroundings. I tripped on a step, and almost crushed the kid. I could have killed him, Randy." His voice rose as he spoke. What about his deficiency was Randy not understanding?

"Again, it was shock. What were you supposed to do?"

"Not drop my kid?"

"But you didn't. Knowing you, you blocked the fall and that's why your ankle was sprained. You're way too hard on yourself."

Flames licked up through his chest. Why was Randy excusing him?

"Stop it." Austin threw his hands in the air. "You are too forgiving of me. Do you know why Cassie hit the deer? Because she told me about getting the job offer and handed me a folder with hours of research she'd done to help *my* ranch, and do you know what I did?"

Randy shook his head.

"Stood there like an idiot. I said nothing. Did nothing. So she left. And I knew she was upset."

Randy lowered his chin and looked at Austin through his lashes. "Did you push the deer in front of her car?"

A low noise erupted from deep in his throat. "You don't get it."

"No, *you* don't get it." His index finger shot like a dagger to him. "So you lock up momentarily when you're dealing with a shock? Lots of people do. But there's no one I'd rather be with in an emergency than you. You act when you need to. When it counts."

"You don't know what you're talking about." He shook his head, not knowing where his brother came up with that whopper.

"What did you do when you found Cassie today?"

"I pried her door open. Checked her for injuries."

"Then what?"

"Called 911." He didn't see where Randy was going with this.

"And?"

"Called you. Called her mom. Checked on AJ." He gulped as he recalled what he'd done next. "Then I got her out of the car. Probably shouldn't have, but I couldn't stand seeing her slumped over the wheel." His throat felt raw just thinking about it. "I stayed with her until the ambulance arrived. Then I drove to the hospital."

"Are you seeing it yet?"

"Seeing what, Randy?" He turned away. He'd only done what anyone would have if they'd driven up.

"You didn't freeze. You acted. You assessed the situation. Made the proper calls. And you followed through."

Austin frowned. He'd never thought of it that way.

"And all those years ago, when I was calling the ambulance, you were closing Dad's eyes and covering his body with the blanket. I remember being glad you were there because I knew you'd do the things I couldn't. And while you didn't tell me every detail of the night in the bar, I can tell you this—if you hadn't been drunk, you would have cleared people out of there the same as Camila did. As for gaining custody of AJ, did you ever stop to think you just tripped? We all do it. I did today. Tripped right over the front step of my store. It happens."

Austin wanted to believe it. Part of him did. He couldn't fault Randy's logic.

"I can see you're overthinking it." Randy patted his shoulder. "You're going to have to let the guilt go. God doesn't want us holding on to our mistakes. That's why He died and rose again. To atone for them. I think you were the one who told me that not too long ago."

He did recognize the words. He'd said them often to his brother over the years. However, it was easier to say them than to apply them to his own life.

"I'm going to take off." Austin stood and hugged Randy, patting his back twice. Then he found AJ in the living room with Hannah, and he plucked the boy off her lap.

"Dada!" AJ grinned, bouncing on his hip.

"How about you and I go home?"

"No." He stuck out his chin and shook his head.

"Yes." Austin ruffled his hair and turned to Hannah. "Thanks for feeding him and entertaining him. I appreciate you always being there for me."

"I love spending time with this little guy." She got up and gave them both a hug.

After he said goodbye to Hannah and Randy, Austin drove home, surprised at how late it was. The day had passed by in an awful blur. He wanted to put it away for good, but he doubted he'd be able to.

Soon, he pulled into his driveway and parked the truck. The night air had a chill to it, reminding him winter would be there before he knew it. He held the boy more closely.

After bathing AJ, wrangling him into pajamas and reading him a story, Austin put him to bed and went to his own room to change into joggers and a T-shirt. Then he peeked into his son's room. He'd already fallen asleep.

Downstairs, Austin stretched out on the couch. Impressions and images of Cassie telling him about her job, then slumped over the steering wheel, then looking so fragile in the hospital—all of them chased around in his mind. Her words echoed through his head.

You're afraid of loving someone and losing them. I get it. But please don't push me away.

Pushing her away. Yeah. She was right about that, but the reasoning? No. Or was she onto something?

And Randy. His words from earlier rushed back. *There's no one I'd rather be with in an emergency but you. You act when you need to. When it counts.*

Had his brother gotten caught up in a delusion? Austin groaned, covering his face with his hands.

God, I'm confused. I want to believe them, but how can I? I've lived with this guilt, this weakness for so long. I'm tired of being weak. Tired of worrying about the next person I'll fail.

Randy's other words came back to him, and they stung in the best possible way.

You're going to have to let the guilt go. God doesn't want us holding on to our mistakes.

If he let go of his mistakes, could he try something new? Like dating? Or marriage? With Cassie?

He wanted something new. He wanted Cassie. *Please, God, help me let the guilt go!*

If he could have Cassie, all his other troubles wouldn't seem so bad. She made everything better. Everything. When he walked in the house and she was there, the atmosphere shimmered like sunshine. Even thinking about the ranch's problems didn't seem so bad when he could discuss them with her.

But how could he look her in the eye and tell her all this after the way he'd treated her today? He'd already told her to go to Colorado, to pursue her dream life. Was he really going to selfishly take it all back?

He let his head fall back on the arm of the couch again and crossed one ankle over the other as he stared up at the ceiling. If the new job and living in the city was her dream, he'd let her go. He'd have to. He loved her too much to hold her back.

But if it wasn't...

He was too tired to think about it anymore. He'd figure it out tomorrow.

Chapter Fourteen

"Mom, can I ask you a question?" Cassie sipped hot tea later that night as she sprawled out on the couch with her back propped up by pillows. She'd been discharged from the hospital earlier, and Mom and Carlos had taken her home. The three of them had talked until an hour ago when he'd left. Cassie liked him more and more the better she got to know him.

Issues were pressing against her heart. Ones she'd been ignoring and suppressing for years—many years.

If she was going to have any shot at the future she wanted—one with a man who loved and appreciated her—she needed answers. And to get them, she had to ask a few difficult questions.

"What is it?" Mom yawned.

"Why did you and Dad break up? I know you said the two of you fell out of love, but there had to be more."

Her mother set her own cup of tea on a coaster. "That's a good question."

Cassie couldn't help holding her breath; the moment felt impossibly charged. She prepared to hear something she might not be able to handle.

"I suppose what I told you wasn't entirely true." Mom folded her hands in her lap.

Here we go. How bad is it going to be?

"I didn't fall out of love with him. He fell out of love with me. I thought we were on the same page when we got married, that we were committed to each other."

"Are you saying he cheated on you?"

"No, not that I know of." She shrugged.

Well, there went that theory. "Then why?"

"He needed attention. A lot of attention. And once I was past the initial phase of thinking he couldn't do anything wrong, I got tired of putting all my energy into his needs. That's when he sought out *new* attention. Your dad was always a flirt, and the flirting ramped up. Made me mad, but I put up with it. And to be fair, I think he struggled with adult responsibilities. The full-time job, the wife, the kid. Maybe it made him feel old. I couldn't really say."

"If that's true, wouldn't he have remained single? I mean, it didn't take him long to find a new wife. He's a father to *her* kids."

"Is he, though?" Mom asked quietly. "Living with kids and being a father to them are two different things. I don't know, Cass. Maybe it was me. He might have gotten tired of me and ended our marriage. I certainly wasn't perfect."

Cassie set the mug on the table, then curled her fingers into the soft throw on her lap. "I always thought he left because of me."

"Why would you think that? He loved you. I don't want you to doubt that."

"I know he loved me when I was little. But after the

divorce, it took no time at all—two years—for him to basically stop communicating with me. Is that love?"

"No," her mother said. "It's not."

"Exactly. And I think I've been trying to find a substitute for him ever since. I just keep falling for the wrong guys."

"Is this about Austin?" Mom's face pinched in confusion.

"No. Maybe. I don't know." She didn't want to tell her mom about James. Didn't want to be judged. Hadn't she judged herself enough as it was? But her defenses were down, and she'd grown closer to her mom this year. "I dated a professor in college. My sophomore year."

Her eyebrows rose to her hairline, but she didn't say anything.

"He was handsome and funny, and he noticed me. Out of all the girls who had crushes on him, he picked me."

Her mother didn't look mad or disappointed. Sad, maybe.

"We snuck around for months. It was exciting, but also frustrating. I wanted us to be official. He led me to believe he wanted the same. Then, right before school let out for the summer, I found out about his fiancée. He denied doing anything wrong. Treated me like a dumb stray who'd followed him home. I realized I'd just been a fling to him. It was humiliating. Devastating."

Cassie smoothed the throw over her lap, comforted by the softness, relieved to have the secret off her chest. "I felt abandoned. Again. And I told myself I wasn't dating older guys anymore. I wanted someone my age who respected me and treated me like I was his equal. And here I am, falling hard for Austin. Same old Cassie."

"Hold up." Mom held out her hand. "The Austin I

know would never disrespect you. Was he rude to you? Or treat you like you're too young for him or something? If he did, I will march right over there and give him a piece of my mind. He has no right. You're a grown woman with a big, beautiful heart and with so much intelligence. He'd be blessed to have you so much as look at him."

The jagged edges of the painful memories softened at her mom's indignation. She kind of wanted to ask her to repeat all those compliments. "Austin didn't treat me any differently than he usually does. He's emotionally unavailable. That's all."

"Well, he's nothing like your father, then. Your dad was emotionally available—to everyone except me." She absentmindedly picked at her sweatshirt. "I could have handled him differently. I think he was insecure...and selfish. Maybe that helps clarify things. Austin isn't insecure, and he's not selfish. I've known him long enough to vouch for that."

"You don't think I've been seeking out a father figure?" *Please, tell me I'm not doomed to be alone.*

"No, I don't. Maybe that's what drew you to the professor in the first place, but if you ask me, it sounds like he was out of bounds, getting attention from young women he had no right even looking at. He was in a position of power, and he abused it."

Her tension slowly eased. "I tried not to put all the blame on him. I think I was afraid of letting myself off the hook."

"I'm sure you could and should have done things differently. I know there are things I wish I'd done better. But this business with the professor, well, it takes two. So stop blaming yourself for what happened with him.

And for what happened with your dad, for that matter. Both men were too self-centered and weak to value what they had in you."

"Thanks, Mom."

"Is there anything else you're blaming yourself about?" Was there? *Yeah*.

She'd wasted her time in Sunrise Bend. She'd secluded herself for the past year instead of making the most of her time here. Turned down invitations and opportunities to build friendships. Gotten too close to AJ when she knew she was only the nanny. And the worst—she'd fallen in love with Austin. She blamed herself for it all.

Pain shot through her temple; whether from regret or the accident, she couldn't be sure.

"When I moved back, I thought Sunrise Bend would be a detour on the way to my dreams, and I'm just now realizing I didn't make much effort to have a life here. All I did was babysit AJ and take care of Gramps."

Mom nodded in understanding. "I should have made sure you were getting out with friends more. I was struggling, too, and I'm sorry."

"You have nothing to be sorry about. You're right—we both struggled. Gramps was such a big part of our lives, and it was hard watching him fade away before our eyes. Even if you would have encouraged me to get out more, I doubt I would have listened."

"'Fade away before our eyes.' That's a good way to put it." Mom tilted her head. "So what changed over the past few weeks? Don't you want to move anymore?"

"I don't know. I've been getting to know all of Austin's friends better, and I fit in with them. Plus, I'm interested in his ranch, how it runs, that sort of thing."

"And the two of you have gotten close." She smiled.

"We have." Cassie nodded. "And I love AJ. I never realized how close we'd become. I love holding him, seeing his eyes light up when we play a game, the feel of his snug little body on my lap. He always reaches up and twists my hair in his fingers when he's tired. And I can't get him to stop calling me mama. I don't even want him to stop."

"He's adorable."

"He is." Cassie sighed. "But Austin's lost so many loved ones. And he's not willing to risk his heart because of it. I really like him—I mean, *really like him*—but at the hospital, he told me to go to Colorado."

She frowned. "He doesn't want you here?"

"He wants me here for AJ. He hasn't made any secret about that. But does he want me here for more? I don't know. I think he's scared. He told me to follow my dreams."

"What if your dreams are right here?"

The million-dollar question. What if all her dreams could come true in Sunrise Bend?

"Mac and Bridget *did* offer me ridiculously low rent for her apartment above the coffee shop."

"Are you seriously thinking about staying?" Her face brightened at the thought.

"It depends." She didn't want to get her mom's hopes up only to disappoint her.

"You're going to have to talk to him. Tell him how you feel. All of it. And spell out what your expectations are. If he can't give you what you're looking for, you should take the job in Colorado. Don't settle. You deserve the life you want."

"You're right." A year ago, she probably couldn't have had this conversation with her mother. And now? It felt good. "I'd hug you, but my neck is killing me, and I don't want to move."

"How about I hug you instead?" She got up, crossed over and wrapped her arms around Cassie before kissing her cheek. "I'm off to bed. Want me to help you to your room?"

"I think I'll sleep out here. I'm already comfortable."

"Are you sure? Do you have enough blankets? Can I get you anything?"

"I'm fine. Good night, Mom. I love you."

"I love you, too."

After her mother retreated to her bedroom, Cassie settled deeper into the couch and let her neck sink into the pillows. What her mom had said earlier about her father and James being self-centered and weak rang true.

Austin was not self-centered.

He was not weak.

But that didn't mean he valued her.

Her eyelids drooped. Exhaustion warred with her wound-up nerves. *Lord, I haven't had a minute to process everything that happened today. Thank You for protecting me. The accident could have been so much worse. I mean, I'd have preferred not having the accident at all, but I can survive bruising, whiplash and a concussion. I'm thankful to be alive.*

Tomorrow would be rough. She had a feeling her entire body would be tight and sore. Plus, she had unfinished business with Austin.

Should she leave it unfinished? What difference would it make if she opened up to him about her feelings? He'd still be too stubborn and scared to let her in.

God, why can't this be easy? I know he likes me. I'm

not imagining that our attraction is mutual. He admit-
ted his feelings run deep. Why won't he take a chance?

A dull ache spread to the back of her head. Great, like
she needed more pain besides the shooting flames in her
temples. All the frustration and insecurity she'd stored
up was threatening to blow.

Do I need to move to have my dream life? Will a cor-
porate job make me feel important?

The pastor's sermon from Sunday replayed in her head
about God wanting people to rely on Him.

Lord, what are You telling me? I know I'm supposed
to rely on You even when it doesn't make sense.

Moving, starting the job, reconnecting with Simone—
all of that made sense.

A drumming sensation in her veins made her close her
eyes. Memories flipped through her mind. She remembered holding AJ for the first time, how the infant had
captured her heart. She remembered making herself at
home in Austin's kitchen, anticipating the moment he'd
return each afternoon. He was reliable. And steady. And
incredibly easy on the eyes.

All the times AJ had fallen and come running to her,
arms wide, for comfort.

All the songs they sang. The games they played. The
quiet moments together.

The horseback ride with Austin showing her around
the ranch, sharing every little detail. All the spreadsheets
she'd created. The gratitude in his eyes when she'd given
him the information to buy more hay.

A business job could never make her feel more important than raising AJ and helping Austin save the ranch.

I am important. Here. Doing exactly what I'm doing.
She settled back into the pillows.

Lord, will You show Austin that he's not to blame for his loved ones' deaths? I don't know why he thinks he freezes in a crisis. Will You get through to him? Please?

As soon as she finished praying, a sense of calmness spread over her body.

She wanted to stay here in Sunrise Bend. To move into the apartment above the coffee shop. To join Austin and his friends on Friday nights. To raise AJ and help Austin with the ranch. To be Austin's girlfriend. She wanted it all.

Tomorrow. She'd tell him everything tomorrow. And if he still pushed her away? Mom was right. She deserved the life she wanted. She wasn't settling for anything less.

Austin set the pen down at the kitchen table and rubbed his eyes. Earlier he'd fallen asleep on the couch and woken with a start around two in the morning. Dawn hadn't yet arrived, but strangely enough, he felt refreshed. More than refreshed. Renewed.

He no longer doubted what to do about his future.

There were no more questions.

He just knew.

The laptop glowed in front of him, and he clicked through the tabs on one of the spreadsheets Cassie had made. Unlike when she'd shown him how to use the software, this time the information made sense. He clicked through the charts. Then he scanned his notes. Finally, he scrawled another equation to estimate his profits if he took a different approach. When he finished, he leaned back and placed both hands behind his head. His upper back muscles stretched, releasing the tension he'd been carrying for months.

This would work.

It had to.

He was buying freezers—for the ranch *and* to sell meat at Randy's store. Yes, he was keeping steers to butcher this winter. Buying more hay. And selling ten percent of his herd to the feedlots. Financially surviving this winter would be tough, but he wasn't afraid anymore.

A sense of accomplishment weaved with hope. He finally had a solid plan for the ranch. A solid plan for his life, too.

He had no intention of letting Cassie go. In a few hours, he was bundling up AJ, dropping him off at Miss Patty's and driving straight to Cassie's. Well…he'd detour to the supermarket and pick up some flowers first. He might be a hopeless bachelor, but even he knew flowers were necessary for the conversation he was planning.

Yesterday, he'd told Cassie to go to Colorado.

Today, he was going to beg her to stay.

Would he be able to change her mind? If only he hadn't been so dumb and scared and stubborn…

Were her feelings for him enough to keep her from moving? If there was the slightest chance she'd stay, he had to try to convince her.

Life was full of risks. Ranching was, too. He'd gotten through hard times with the good Lord's help, and he'd enjoyed good times, too. This drought would pass, and he'd have a story to pass on to AJ when he was old enough to take over the ranch. Maybe it would give his son the courage to try new solutions rather than plod along, feeling doomed.

And if everything went well today, Austin wouldn't be alone for the ride.

A nervous sense of anticipation zipped through him as he thought of telling Cassie about his plan. He could picture the two of them sitting right here at this table, deciding which of the logos she'd drawn up would be best. They'd review her charts and come up with new ways to help the ranch. The woman seemed to have a knack for finding ways around the impossible.

He pictured other things, too. Him wrapping her in his arms and lifting her off her feet to kiss her until she was dizzy. Asking her to show him the spreadsheet one more time just to watch her get all serious as she pointed to the screen.

Yeah, she was the partner he wanted. The one he needed. He could only hope she agreed.

He hadn't made it easy on himself. Hadn't given her many reasons to take a chance on him. But he had to try. He'd get down on his knees if necessary.

He loved her. And he was ready to say the three little words he'd never uttered to a woman before.

I love you, Cassie.

He just hoped she loved him, too.

Chapter Fifteen

⟨⟩

Cassie opened one eyelid. Then the other. Stretched her right arm over her head. *Ouch.* Stretched the left over, too. *Double ouch.* Sunlight streamed through the picture window onto the floor. She propped herself up on her elbows, squinting as the blood rushed to her head. Sleeping on the couch probably hadn't been the best idea. She ached everywhere.

What time was it? She reached down for her phone, but her hand only met carpet. Moving her fingers around, she finally gripped it and brought it up to her face as she let her head drop back into the pillows.

She'd slept almost eight hours. Not bad.

Slowly, she sat up for real this time. Waited a few minutes for her equilibrium to return, then swung her legs over the side of the couch and picked her way to the bathroom. Her image in the mirror made her flinch.

Swollen eyes, bruises and a bandage above her left temple didn't scream beauty queen. After brushing her teeth and showering, she changed into joggers and a soft sweater and promptly returned to the couch.

How could something as simple as a shower completely exhaust her? She drew the throw over her body and reclined back, eyes closed, not able to keep a thought in her head.

Two sharp knocks on the front door disrupted her rest. She wanted to shout *go away* but forced herself to get up and see who it was. Maybe Mom had forgotten her keys or something. Not that she'd be up this early. Since she worked second shift, she got home around midnight and slept late each morning.

Two more knocks revved up her irritation. "I'm coming."

Flinging open the door, she froze.

Austin stood there with a vase full of dark pink roses and a white paper bag she recognized from the bakery dangling from his hand. The other hand balanced two cups of coffee, one on top of the other.

His mouth spread into the widest grin she'd ever seen. Even the corners of his eyes crinkled. "Hey."

"Hey." Why did she feel so shy? She hugged her arms around her waist and cocked her head to the side and back. "Want to come in?"

"Yeah." He entered, and she padded back to the couch, sitting and bringing one ankle under the other knee. Austin set the flowers on the coffee table, then handed her the top to-go cup. "This is for you."

"Thanks." She held it between her hands, enjoying the warmth as her mind raced with questions. Why was he here? Obviously to check on her. A natural thing to do after the accident. And the flowers? Guilt offering, most likely. If he told her to move to Colorado again, so help her...

No, Cassie. No. Last night, you prayed, and you know

what you have to do. Even if it's difficult. Especially if it's difficult. Tell him how you feel. All of it.

"How are you doing this morning?" His gray eyes glistened with concern. He'd taken a seat in the armchair, and he was leaning forward, coffee in one hand as he studied her. "Are you in pain?"

"A little." She nodded. "The shower helped. I'm mostly just tired."

"I can imagine."

A charged silence fell, and Cassie scrambled to figure out what she wanted to say to him and how to say it. She took the lid off the coffee, blew across the surface of the steaming brew and tentatively took a sip.

Although he'd hurt her yesterday, she felt nothing but love for him. But she couldn't just blurt out that she loved him. She needed to articulate her thoughts as well as spell out her expectations. Find out if he had it in him to try to meet them. Assure him she'd do everything in her power to meet his needs, too.

"I did a lot of thinking after I left the hospital." Austin had a humble assuredness about him. He projected confidence, and she hoped it meant this conversation would go well. "About what you said. About what I said."

"I did, too." The hoarseness of her voice made her take another sip of coffee. Hot, but necessary. Much better.

"You're right," he said. "I've lost a lot of people I loved. I put up walls, and I told myself it was because I was useless in an emergency, but I don't know if that's true. Not anymore, at least."

She nodded. She didn't know how else to respond.

"Take the accident yesterday. Randy helped me see that I jumped into action when it mattered. When I arrived, I checked to make sure you were breathing. Called

911. Called Randy. Called your mom. Got you out of the car—if I caused your neck and back to be hurt worse, I sincerely apologize."

"You didn't." Her nerves bunched as she thought of him arriving at the scene and doing all that. "The X-rays showed no damage beyond the normal strain an accident like this would cause."

"Good." He nodded, setting his cup on the coffee table. "When you were in my arms, it destroyed me. Brought me right back to the day my father died. Brought me back to Camila's apartment when I realized I could have been shot and that *I* should have been the one saving her, not the other way around. Brought me back to standing in front of the social worker with AJ in my arms and realizing I was the boy's entire world. Me. A cowboy who'd never once held a baby. In charge of a three-month-old child."

"I never realized..." She'd taken the events at face value, not delving beneath the surface layer to consider how Austin had been forced to emotionally deal with the tragedies. "You always seem so calm and in control. It's easy to think nothing rattles you, you know?"

"You think so?" A lopsided grin briefly graced his mouth. "I must put on a mask then, because things rattle me. The thought of losing you yesterday—it rattled me."

"Then why did you tell me to leave? To go to Colorado?" Even saying the words brought on the sensation of impending tears. "Why do you push me away?"

He sat back, frowning. "Will you think I'm a loser if I admit I'm scared?"

That brought a chuckle. "No. I don't think you're a loser."

"Good." He nodded, smiling. "I'm used to pushing

people away if they get too close. I can handle friendship. But I avoid anything more. And all these big life-changing decisions hit me at once. I couldn't handle them."

She could sympathize. He did have a lot going on, and she did, too. It was overwhelming.

"I'm sorry for hurting you, Cassie. Deep down, I knew I'd deal with the ranch and AJ—I had to. It was you leaving that threw me over the edge."

The words he was saying, the way he was looking at her... Dare she get her hopes up?

"You see, when I come in every afternoon, I know a couple of things." He lifted his index finger. "AJ will be blissfully asleep upstairs in his crib, and you'll be sitting on your stool, sipping tea from your favorite mug and scrolling on your phone."

She cringed. He stated it like it was a good thing, but it sounded boring.

"I can count on it." He got a faraway look in his eyes. "The house will feel warm, and it has nothing to do with the temperature outside. Because after I wash up in the mudroom, I'll walk into the kitchen, and you'll look up at me with that big smile of yours and my life will feel right. I'll know that everything will be okay, even if it's falling apart."

"That doesn't make sense."

"I know it doesn't." His smile grew wider. "That's the beauty of it. I finally understand why all my friends got married. You were right, Cassie, about needing a partner to weather life's storms. I've been weathering them by myself for too long, and I haven't done a very good job."

As much as she wanted to shout that she loved him

and needed him, she couldn't. Not until she had answers to the other questions.

"When you asked for my business help, I know it was to keep me on as the nanny. But I've got to be honest with you. It hurt that you didn't show much interest in the spreadsheets I created. And you wouldn't even consider the idea in that article. Don't you respect my opinion?"

"You're right. I didn't give your ideas a fair shake."

Just as she'd thought. Why it hurt so much to hear him affirm it, she didn't know.

"As for the spreadsheets." He shook his head, his face beaming in wonder. "They intimidated me. I can check emails, shop online and that's about it. You're over there whipping through graphs and formulas and tabs and all the other stuff I'd never learned."

"But you didn't use them." She gave him a pointed stare. "It was a waste of time."

"That's what you think." He shifted to the edge of the chair, and his knee grazed hers. "I used them. Last night. And everything you'd printed that was in the folder, too. I've got a plan for the ranch—a hybrid of your plan. I never would have been able to come up with it on my own. Honestly, the fact you did all that research convinced me I could try something different."

"What are you saying?"

"I'm trying a new strategy this winter. I'm dipping my toes into selling my beef directly to buyers. I'm ordering several freezers for the ranch. Randy's keeping two in his store to sell beef to his customers. The butchers you listed—I'm calling them today. I've already selected the steers I'm keeping this winter. And I'm buying more hay if I can find it."

"So you're not selling off more cattle?" She couldn't believe he was actually taking her advice.

"I have to sell some of them, and I've made peace with it. I simply can't feed them all this winter. And if money gets tight, I'll unload trucks on weekends at the grocery store. I'm not losing my ranch."

He sounded confident. *Thank You, Lord. You got through to him.*

"And Cassie, I'm not losing you, either." He plucked the coffee cup out of her hand and set it on the end table. Then he took her hand in his. "Not if I can help it."

The words poured over her, soothing her fears, raising her hopes to new heights.

"I don't want you to move to Colorado." His eyes bore into hers. "I want you to stay."

Austin watched for any sign he'd gotten through to her. He hadn't told her everything on his mind, but he would.

"What would my role be if I stayed?" She spoke quietly, her gaze clear and open. He hated to see the bruises on her face, but a wave of gratitude surged inside him that she was here—banged up, yes, but alive and well.

"Your role?" Here it was. The opening he needed. "Those storms to weather? I need a partner for them. I hope you'll consider dating me. I want you to be my girlfriend."

The way her eyelashes fluttered, he wasn't sure if he'd made her mad, sad or what.

"I love you, Cassie." He got up to sit next to her on the couch, smooshing close, putting his arm around her shoulders.

She shifted, and her face was close to his, so close he

could feel her warm breath on his cheeks. "Is this another step in your Operation Make Cassie Stay?"

"Okay, I deserve that. But no, this isn't about AJ. It's about me. And you. Look, I love you, and I'll hire Allison tomorrow if you don't want to take care of AJ anymore. I'll still want you to stay. I'll still love you. I mean, I get it that you want to work and use your degree. I want what's best for you. Because whatever is best for you is best for me, too. I want you to be happy."

"You really mean it?" A tear slid down her cheek, and he used his thumb to gently wipe it away.

"I really mean it."

"I love you, too, Austin." Her voice broke. "I want to stay. I want to date you. I want…forever. If that scares you, tell me now, because I'm not going to be content with a lukewarm relationship. I want to get married." She looked like she couldn't believe she'd admitted it. "Not tomorrow or anything."

"Tomorrow might be rushing it." He chuckled, pulling her closer. "I want forever, too. I hope you'll continue giving me your advice about the ranch, no matter if you find a job or not. You make me see possibilities I didn't know existed."

"You really mean it, don't you?" Her eyes glimmered with love.

"I do. And you have my word I'll always treat you with the respect you deserve. You're one of a kind, and you're way too smart and beautiful for a rancher like myself, but boy, Cassie, I love you. I'd do just about anything for you."

She threw her arms around his neck and pressed her mouth to his. He froze, shocked, then slid his hands around her back and matched her kiss. He took it slow, wanting to show her how much he cared, how valuable she was to him. And her kiss gave him the same feeling as seeing her at the kitchen counter each day.

He'd found the woman who made him whole, the one who brought warmth to his cold life, the one who made him feel safe, the one he wanted to protect.

"Cassie," he said breathlessly.

"Uh-huh?" Her forehead was pressed to his, and it was all he could do not to start kissing her again.

"Say it again." He needed to hear her say the words he'd heard so few times in his life.

"I love you." Her mouth arched into a smile. "I love you, Austin."

"I love you, too."

"I already have ideas for how to keep track of the steers you keep and the meat you sell."

"Of course, you do." He laughed, giving her a light kiss on the lips. "See? This is why I can't live without you."

"You just want me for my spreadsheet skills, don't you?" she teased.

"Your spreadsheets, your smile, your wisdom, your kiss. I want it all." He held her gaze with his.

"You've got it, cowboy. I'm all yours."

Epilogue

This was the easiest decision he'd made in years, and it was almost time to make it official. Austin opened the side door to his farmhouse with a tad too much force. Operation Make Cassie Stay would be permanently retired tonight.

He took off his outerwear and washed his hands as he stared out the window over the utility sink where snow fell outside. Christmas was in one week, and he'd decided he couldn't wait until Christmas Eve like he'd originally planned. No, he was asking Cassie to marry him today. The ring was upstairs in a box next to the outfit he'd ironed last night. He'd take a quick shower, change and get everything ready—if he didn't pass out from nerves first.

It was a good thing it was Saturday. Hannah and Randy had dropped off supplies earlier and taken AJ home with them for a sleepover. Which meant Austin could devote all his attention to Cassie. To proposing.

Forever with her was so close he could taste it.

Fifteen minutes later, he was showered and dressed, ring in pocket. With supper warming in the oven, he got to work setting the table. It took him three tries to light the candles his hands were shaking so hard. Then he moved the vase of flowers to the table, unboxed the small chocolate cake and grinned as he read the icing.

Will You Marry Me?

He fumbled to get the ring box out of his pocket, opened it and stared at the classic diamond engagement ring he'd picked out. It was small, the best he could afford. He hoped she wouldn't mind. Then he snapped the box shut and slipped it back into his pocket.

The sound of Cassie's car alerted him that she'd arrived, and his heartbeat thumped as the engine went silent.

God, please let her say yes.

His friends had given him terrible advice last week when he'd told them he was proposing. He hoped he hadn't given them as dumb ideas for their proposals as they'd tossed out to him.

Randy had told him to borrow a life jacket from his store and tell her she was his lifesaver. *Ick.*

Blaine and Jet had gotten way too excited about a cockamamie scheme of a scavenger hunt through the stables and barns. Didn't they understand the smell of manure wasn't romantic? And hello, it was freezing outside.

Mac wasn't any better. Ballroom dancing in his pole barn? Had the man lost his mind? And Sawyer, still in a daze from Tess having their baby—a girl named Kinsey—had said, "I don't know. Maybe take her out to dinner or something." At which Austin had replied, "Where? To Bubba's for barbecue?" It was the closest thing to fine dining Sunrise Bend had, and it would not do.

No. Just no.

The side door opened, and he held his breath, listening as her steps drew near. And there she was. Wearing a little black dress that made him gulp. Her hair curled loosely around her face and her smile gave him heart palpitations. He'd told her he was making her a fancy dinner. The dress she was wearing wouldn't do it justice.

"Well, hey there, beautiful." He wrapped his hands around her waist and drew her to him, kissing her with gusto.

"My, my." She fanned herself. Her cheeks were deliciously rosy. "Hey there yourself, handsome."

"Hard day at work?" He kept a light hold on her waist.

"Yes, my boss is demanding."

"Oh, yeah?" He took her by the hand and led her to the table.

"Yeah. He expects me to take care of his toddler all week *and* track the sales of his beef on my time off."

"Tell him you deserve a raise."

"I deserve a raise." She arched her eyebrows, her eyes dancing in delight.

"You got it."

"What's all this?" She looked around the table. "You really are making a fancy dinner, aren't you?"

"I do my best." His pulse started sprinting, making his body feel like it was going haywire.

There was no way he'd be able to get through the meal with his nerves this messed up. He made a split-second decision to start with dessert…and the proposal.

"Take a seat." He held out a chair for her, letting his fingers graze her shoulders. Then he went to the kitchen and carried the cake to the table. He didn't set it in front of her, though. Not yet.

Instead, he took a deep breath and tried to remember the speech he'd rehearsed.

Nothing. Couldn't remember a single word.

He'd have to wing it.

Austin walked back and offered her his hand. She gave him a curious look and let him help her to her feet.

"What's going on? You're acting really weird."

"Yeah. I am." Why deny it? "Cassie, these months we've been together have been the best I can remember. The ranch is doing better than I thought possible before I asked for your help. I mean, it's still struggling, but I'm not worried about losing it anymore."

"I know." She touched his cheek, her eyes tender.

"The beef is selling great." He still couldn't believe how much business he'd gotten from Randy's store. Some of the customers were having him ship it directly to them on dry ice every month. "And thanks to you, I have enough hay to squeak through winter, God willing."

"You work hard, Austin. You deserve the credit, not me."

"No, you definitely deserve the credit. I didn't bring you here to talk about the ranch, though. Not AJ, either, although you're the only mom he's ever known and I'm glad you've stopped trying to get him to call you Cassie. You're his mama. He knows it. I know it."

Her brown eyes filled with tears, and she smiled. "I love him, Austin."

"I know." He tightened his hold on her hands. "I was going to wait until Christmas Eve, but I can't wait another day. You brought light to my dim world. You make my senses come alive. Your presence in this house makes it warm and inviting, like cinnamon rolls and coffee on a cold morning."

He let go of her hands and went over to where he'd left the cake. Then he brought it over, set it next to her and got on one knee. "You're the sweetest thing I've ever seen. I love you more every day. I need you. AJ needs you. This ranch needs you. Will you marry me?"

She glanced at the cake, her lips moving as she read the icing. Her eyes grew round, then she brought her fingers to her lips. Tears slid down her cheeks as she nodded. He took out the ring and slid it on her finger, and rose when it was on.

"You mean it?" he asked.

"Of course, I mean it! Yes, I'll marry you." She hugged him tightly, and he kissed her. Thoroughly. Then he helped her sit back down in the chair, and her smile full of delight made him grin.

"Um, are we not having supper, Austin?" She swiped a finger full of icing from the bottom of the cake. "Mmm... chocolate. My favorite."

"Yes, we're having supper. Unless you want to skip it and just have cake?" He bent to kiss her cheek.

She turned at the last minute and met his lips with hers. If they kept this up, they'd never eat supper. But who was he to complain?

"I don't care if I ever eat real food again as long as you're in my arms," he said.

"Deal." She grinned. "I can't believe we're going to get married."

"I can't believe you said yes."

"I can't believe we haven't cut that cake."

He laughed. "Coming right up."

* * * * *

*If you enjoyed this Wyoming Ranchers book, pick up
the previous titles in Jill Kemerer's miniseries:*

The Prodigal's Holiday Hope
A Cowboy to Rely On
Guarding His Secret
The Mistletoe Favor
Depending on the Cowboy

Available now from Love Inspired!

Dear Reader,

My heart is overflowing with gratitude. I can't believe this is the final book in the Wyoming Ranchers series. I've loved writing these stories, and I knew from the start that Austin's journey would be special.

Austin faced many problems in every area of his life, and the one thing going right suddenly went wrong—Cassie. He had to face a lot of fears, and I was so happy when he finally got over his misconception of himself and got the guts to leave his comfort zone to fight for Cassie and the ranch.

Cassie doubted herself, too, especially her romantic choices. Yes, she had good reasons for those doubts, but Austin helped her see what she really wanted, and it wasn't a corporate job far away. Sometimes everything we want is right there in front of us…if we're brave enough to admit it.

I hope you enjoyed this book and the Wyoming Ranchers series. I love connecting with readers. Feel free to email me at jill@jillkemerer.com or write me at P.O. Box 2802, Whitehouse, Ohio, 43571.

Wishing you every blessing,
Jill Kemerer

COMING NEXT MONTH FROM
Love Inspired

THEIR ROAD TO REDEMPTION
by Patrice Lewis

Leaving his shameful past behind, Thomas Kemp joins a newly formed Amish community in Montana. It's not long before he meets young widow Emma Fisher and her toddler daughter. Their bond could mean the family that Thomas has always wanted—but can he keep his past from ruining their future?

A CONVENIENT AMISH BRIDE
by Lucy Bayer

Grieving widower David Weiss has no plans of finding love again, but when local woman Ruby Kaufmann offers comfort to his daughter, they agree to a marriage of convenience. They both decide to keep their hearts out of the arrangement, but it isn't long before that promise starts to unravel...

THE NURSE'S HOMECOMING
True North Springs • by Allie Pleiter

After ending her engagement, Bridget Nicholson returns home to figure out the rest of her life. So she takes on a job as Camp True North Springs' temporary nurse. The last thing she expects is to find old love Carson Todd also working there. Will it derail her plans, or could he be what she's been searching for all along?

A COWBOY FOR THE SUMMER
Shepherd's Creek • by Danica Favorite

All that stands between Isaac Johnston and running his own camp is an internship with rival Abigail Shepherd at her family's horse farm. The problem is, he's terrified of horses. Can Abigail help Isaac overcome his fears and prove there is more to them—and her—than meets the eye?

THE BABY SECRET
by Gabrielle Meyer

Arriving a few days early to her sister's wedding, Emma Holt hopes to relax after a tragic end to her marriage. When she meets best man Clay Foster and his baby daughter, things start to look up—until she discovers a secret about his baby that could tear them apart...

THE WIDOW'S CHOICE
by Lorraine Beatty

Widow Eden Sinclair wants nothing to do with her bad boy brother-in-law, Blake Sinclair. When he comes home unexpectedly, she fears the shock will be too much for his ill father to handle. Then she discovers why Blake really came back. It might threaten her family—and her heart as well.

LOOK FOR THESE AND OTHER LOVE INSPIRED BOOKS WHEREVER BOOKS ARE SOLD, INCLUDING MOST BOOKSTORES, SUPERMARKETS, DISCOUNT STORES AND DRUGSTORES.

LICNM0523

HARLEQUIN
PLUS

Try the best multimedia subscription service for romance readers like you!

Read, Watch and Play.

Experience the easiest way to get the romance content you crave.

Start your **FREE TRIAL** at
www.harlequinplus.com/freetrial.